THINGS MAGICAL UNDER THE MOON

A GRIM ANTHOLOGY

ALEXIS L CARROLL

AMANDA STOCKTON

This is a work of fiction. All of the characters, organizations, and events portrayed in this anthology are products of the authors' imaginations.

THINGS MAGICAL UNDER THE MOON: A GRIM ANTHOLOGY

Published and formatted in coordination with BatwordsMedia

www.batwordsmedia.com

ISBN

Print 979-8-9885416-0-8

E-book 979-8-9885416-1-5

First Edition: August 31, 2023

Cover art by Real Life Design Covers

Custom interior graphics by Amanda Stockton

To all the strange ones under the moon

CONTENTS

THE UNTAMED DAUGHTER

AMANDA STOCKTON

Songs of judgment chorused from the pews of the crows, and I waited. I remembered the moonlight. How it had glowed in the darkness before darkness was all I had. Before my eyes were taken and I was abandoned in the woods to die a broken woman. I didn't remember how I'd gotten there. How I'd become this emptied vessel.

Exposed beyond my nakedness, dozens of corvid eyes pierced me, scrutinizing my every breath. I wouldn't cry when they'd come. I wouldn't fight or plead. Death is not so easily swayed. Instead, I would welcome them. Let them strip away the sinew that bound me to this cold place. Until all that was left of me was in the bellies of the crows, and I could fly.

I brought my hands to my face. They hovered in space, too afraid to touch my own cheeks—to lay a hand on ruin. To be reminded of what once was, and what could never be again.

I waited, felt the wind of flight blow against my exposed flesh as the crows swooped over me, one after another. But no beaks or talons tore me open. The ending I'd been waiting for didn't come.

"What are you waiting for?" I screamed. The earth rose up from beneath me, sent my knees into the brambles. I beat my fists down into the thorns. The jagged edges of earth tore at my flesh, ripped me open. Pushing myself back to my feet, I stomped, kicked, and I screamed my throat raw. I laid waste to what was meant to be my grave. Until the wet-warmth of blood ran down my legs and slicked my toes. I screamed again, "Why won't you end this?"

The crows answered with silence. I tried to see. But my eyes were gone. Taken . . . or given away, I couldn't remember. Again, my hands hovered over my face, trapping the scent of blood. I cried. Though if it were tears or blood weeping from where my eyes ought to have been, I couldn't tell.

I cried myself empty until the day gave way to the coldness of the night. I wrapped my arms around myself and thought of that moon. Its shine and fullness filled my dreams. Its phasing parts exploded into a murder of crows, down to its last crescent. And then it, too, fell away to black-feathered darkness.

I woke, but it didn't feel like waking. I was trapped in a dark nightmare where I had become hollow and unnatural. My body shook against the chilled breezes of flight that rushed across me. The crows spoke their counsel, each giving testimony through fallen feathers laid upon my flesh. Soon, there were enough feather offerings to keep out the cold.

"It's time to get up," called a feminine voice, both familiar and unfamiliar. I ignored it, but it called again. "You need to get up. Now."

"I can't," my voice cracked.

"You can. You will. Stand up."

Though I wanted to lie in my nest of feathers and ruin forever, I lifted my head from the dirt.

"Stand up." Her gentle command moved my bones. My feet found their hold beneath me. I stood. The crow feathers didn't fall from my skin. Instead, they clung to me like tender armor. A warm and structural embrace that kept me standing when I so badly wanted, again, to fall. I stood as what must have looked like a frightening beast of a woman—a girl—a small child left to rot. All mud and blood and gore wrapped in feathers.

Something reached out and touched my fingers. I shuddered and pulled my hand away.

"I won't hurt you. Not ever again." The voice—familiar and unfamiliar—was closer. "Reach out your hand if you're ready to leave this place."

I trembled. Some small part of me thought perhaps it was Death speaking, waiting to take my hand and lead me away from life itself. And more, I wondered how it was possible—as someone who had recently begged for death—that I was so afraid and unwilling to follow.

She said nothing. But she was there. I could feel her. A warmth radiated from her skin, the sweetness of hyacinth perfumed her hair. I reached out my hand, and she took it in hers. I let out a breath of relief and inhaled, unsure of how long it was since someone had last touched me so carefully. She led me forward, and I trusted her—this stranger in the woods. I didn't know how long we walked together in silence; her holding my hand, acting as my eyes. By the time we came to a stop, the ground beneath my toes felt of dry grass.

"You must go on from here, alone," she said. Her voice

was softer, as if she was trying hard to mask some unknown pain.

"I don't even know your name."

Her free hand cupped my cheek, and for the smallest moment, it felt as though I would never again feel fear or loneliness or despair. "My name does not matter. For I am nothing and no one. Just a girl in the wood, far from castles and dreams. I run with the wolves. I sing with the crows. For I am an untamed daughter, wild as flame, I burn."

"Untamed daughter?" Her touch had gone before the words made it from my lips. Leaving me, once again, to the mercy of the woods. I did as she'd bidden and walked onward. The path started smoothly enough. Then it twisted, turned, and dropped out from under me altogether. I tumbled, rolled down a hill, unable to stop myself. Only doing so by a violent collision between my ribs and a boulder. My feathered armor held me tight when my bones should have broken, but it couldn't keep the breath within me. I writhed in pain when I tried to pull in air.

I found it. My breath, my life, my will to stand again. Only now, I didn't know what direction I was facing. Fear of taking the wrong step kept me locked in place. I stayed by the rock that nearly killed me, and I clung to it for life. Like a buoy in a turbulent sea.

Something was moving. Footsteps, quick and light-weight. Panting. A low, deep-throated growl that soon turned into a howl. As a child, they taught me a wolf howling was calling for its pack. Lost or found, that wolf cried a call so ear-piercing, I had to cover mine. Staying put was not an option. I had to move.

The sun's warmth found my face, and I used it as a guide. I kicked stones with my bare feet, tripped on fallen trees, and got caught in monstrously large spider webs.

They covered my face, scratched against my ears. Tiny little legs scurried across my neck. I smacked them away, clawed at myself, shook my whole body trying to be rid of the hellish things.

I dropped my hands to my sides, dug my fingers into my feather armor, and I screamed. A scream that tugged at every fiber of my being. Everything I used to be was tied up in that scream, and I let it all go. Like I could float away on the echoes of my pain and be free from that dreadful place.

My feet remained planted on the ground. The same ground that carried the wolves closer. They heard me. Must have—my howling at the sky. I was lost, and the pack approached. I heard one of them close by, panting. Its feet moved swiftly through the brush. I started to run. It started to run. Somewhere behind me, two sets of feet, one on my left and one—no, two—on my right. I ran. It didn't matter what direction anymore. I just needed to run.

Wings flapped by my ear. The wind of flight graced my skin. The crows called, led me onward. They wove through the trees and I followed, echoing their song.

We broke into a clearing and the crows circled around me, halting my haste altogether. One landed on my shoulder and nudged me with its beak.

"What is it?" I asked, out of breath. "The wolves . . . we mustn't stop."

But the bird simply nudged me again. I listened, waited for the inevitability of claws and teeth and more howling that never came. My breathing calmed, and I caught the most wonderful smell of bread and bacon on the cook.

"Hello?" I called out and continued forward, led by my hungry belly and hope. What a funny thing, hope. The way it causes us to move when we ought not to. I called out again. My voice high, scratching at my throat.

A crow was all that answered. I followed and stumbled into a gate. After fumbling around for a moment, I managed to find and lift the lever. The bird led me to a door. I knocked. At first, timidly. Then I beat my palms and fists into the wood grain, letting my hopeful desperation take complete control.

The door swung open. "Oh, thank the gods." I let out a whimper that bordered on laughter, overjoyed by the idea that I would finally be safe.

"What the bleeding hell?" It was a man's voice that answered my call. He rushed me in the door and closed it behind us. "Of all the sights in these woods, I dare say you're the most wild I've ever seen. What on earth happened to ye, child?"

"It's a terribly long story," I replied. "But I will tell you. If perhaps, that is—do you think you could spare a bite of bread?"

"Oh me. My manners. Of course. Of course. I'll get you some, with honey."

"That would be delightful. Thank you."

He directed me to a seat. The soft leather chair he'd placed me in held my body in a firm embrace. His footsteps fell heavily on the wood floor as he left to fetch the bread. Perhaps with futility, I patted down my feather armor. A will to improve my appearance as an unexpected dinner guest. Bread and honey filled the air. But there was something under it. Another scent, familiar and unfamiliar, that tainted the sweetness of the food. I thought to sniff myself, but I only carried the smell of the forest on my skin.

The man returned, placed a plate of bread and honey on my lap and a glass of milk in my hand. He settled on a seat across from me. "What the devil happened to ye?" There was something in his voice that almost sounded serene.

I wiped milk from my lip. "I–I don't . . . I don't quite remember." But I did my best to explain how an eyeless girl stumbled through the woods and found herself breaking bread with a kindly stranger.

"A sight you are," he said, putting more bread in my empty hand. "You'll stay here. Eat."

Of course, I ate it. I was half-starved. Though the honey was different from what I'd known before. I couldn't place it, the extra taste. Was it lavender? My lips went numb. So did my fingers. I wasn't sure if I ever felt my toes. My body stiffened. Then I couldn't move my fingers at all. They just hung there in front of me. Until all my parts joined in frozen mutiny. I couldn't even speak. First my eyes and now my voice . . . my body.

"Oh good. How lovely to see it already working." The man's voice was darker then, like the shadow of a thorn. "Very seldom do young women come directly to me. As it is, I must always hunt for them myself." His boots thudded on the floor. So much heavier than they'd previously been. "While I do enjoy hunting, there is something uniquely special about fowl seeking me out."

I begged my body to move, to scream, to do anything besides just sit there. But sit there was all I could do. He put a hand on my wrist, and my stomach curled. Still, I could not move, or fight, or beg.

"We are going to have a lot of fun," he said. And I could practically hear the smile twist on his face, cold and jagged like a rusty blade. His hand moved up my arm, inspecting my feather armor. He lingered a bit too long over my heart. Something swung down and struck my chest. But it couldn't penetrate the feathers. No matter how hard he pulled, or pried, or tried to cut, the armor stayed intact. "An interesting bit of magic. I suspect you left out a few details of your story. Tricky. Tricky, indeed. What are we going to do about this?"

He crouched in front of me, the leather of his boots creaking as he did. "Hmm." He thrummed his fingers on my knee, keeping tempo for his thoughts. I ached to know what dark things dwelled in his pondering and paled under my own assumptions. "Might work. What do I do with you while I pull it together?"

I couldn't answer him. Not that he'd actually asked me. No matter how badly I wanted to sink my teeth into his throat, I remained still. I had no voice. No body. Just a mind trapped in a sightless, fleshy cage.

Boots and floorboards creaked when he stood upright again. His heavy steps left the room somewhere behind me. No concern about the living statue escaping. My muscles burned with constriction. Not having eyes didn't stop me from seeing what a fool I'd been. I cursed myself in my screaming mind. Begged myself to move my body, to flee, to escape, to live. But there was nothing but stillness from me. Nothing but quiet, motionless self-betrayal.

Moments later, he returned. Something heavy and metal dragged along the wooden floor behind him. With a clank, a shackle latched around my ankle.

"You're going to be a good girl while I'm out," he said, running a finger down the bridge of my nose. "Stay put." The front door opened and locked shut behind him.

Tears broke through my scabbing wounds and rolled down my cheeks. The crows, dozens or more, called from outside the door. What could they want? They were the ones that brought me here. But why? Maybe I was wrong when I thought they'd pardoned me back in the forest. Why save me? Why coat me in armor just to deliver me to the devil?

Glass shattered somewhere close. Crows burst into the cabin, swarmed around me. Feathers and wings and beaks flocked and stirred the air. A deafening cyclone whipped around and chilled me. This time, they were not laying more armor. Far from it. They pecked at my hands. Lacerated my forehead. Tore me open. Violent blooms of blood overran my fingers. It spilled down my arms, and still, they swarmed.

"Stop it!" I screamed, surprised to find my voice. My hands pulled into my chest, and I was alive again. The birds flew back out the window. All except one. He led me, as before. Called me toward the door. I found my feet, shuffled across the floor, broken glass bit my toes, but it couldn't slow me. Not now. Not then. Not whilst knowing what was to come.

I walked with my hands stretched out before me, feeling for the door, found the handle, and pulled it open. My crow flew over my shoulder, back outside. I rushed to follow, only to be yanked back by the chain still stuck to my ankle. Powered by all the momentum of my eagerness to escape, my upper body slammed into the ground. I tried to catch myself, pad my landing, but my hand caught under my chin on its side. My pinky finger snapped backward under my colliding weight. I yelped, cried, cradled my hand. But only for a moment before the pain turned to rage, and I grasped at the chain bound to my ankle and pulled. My hands and arms shook under the strain of my effort to force my foot through the shackle. All it did was shave off layers of skin until a hot slick greased its metal. Still, it would not come free.

"A key," I breathlessly instructed the crow. "We need a key."

He took flight. I followed his calls to another door,

found the handle, and went inside. There it was. That smell once hidden under the bread and honey, familiar and unfamiliar. It slapped me in the face. Rot. It was the familiar scent of death. Once you've walked with Death, begged for him to take you away from all the pain and loneliness of the world, you recognize his smell. But this was worse than I'd ever experienced. The odor was thick in the air, suffocating. That man was the devil, and this was hell. I retched on the floor.

The bird called. I wiped my mouth and found the crow at a small table. It pulled on my index finger, urging my movement. I reached and—recoiled. Pulled away. No. This was wrong. The crow grabbed my hair, pulled my face to the table, and then nudged the thing toward me. It rolled toward my empty eye socket. I shook my head in protest. The crow squawked and pulled at my feather armor, still secure.

"Oh. Of course," I murmured, remembering where my trust belonged. I picked the wet orb up in one hand, the crow dropped another in my other hand. Admittedly, I didn't know what to do next. My hands shook and I almost dropped one. My crow perched on my shoulder, squawking out orders that I didn't understand how to follow. I didn't want to . . . It couldn't be that easy.

Tapping paws slowly clicked on the floor, approaching me. A deep, low growl rumbled from a wolf's belly. My hands lurched, dropping what each held. The crow pulled my hair, urging me toward the floor to pick them up again. But I couldn't. I couldn't see the point in fighting anymore. The wolf pack or the man, it didn't matter. I couldn't see any hope for me. I couldn't see.

I couldn't see.

The tapping of paws grew nearer. The crow yanked on

my hair. I bid to scream when the wolf barked through sopping jaws. Dropping to my knees, at the continued pull of the crow, I hastened my blind search for what I'd dropped. As soon as I found them again, hot breath met me face-to-face. The wolf's nose barely touched my own. Its growl receded as it sniffed what rolled around in my palms. It panted, turning its nose back to my face. Whined.

A long, flat tongue brushed my cheek, forcing a restrained sob to escape through my teeth. The wolf whined again. She licked the tears and crusted blood from my face with a surprising gentleness. And without any thought or reason I could explain, I wrapped my arms around the wolf's neck and wept into her fur. Her head nuzzled against me, her way of embracing me back. I could breathe again, easier than I had all day or night or however long it had been since my eyes were taken and I was left as a feast for the crows.

But I had not been so easily disposed. And in my hands, I held the next step of reclamation, should I choose to take it.

My fingers curled around my prize. The crow called from somewhere nearby. I raised my hands as if in prayer and pressed them both into place.

I opened my eyes to see my own blurred hands, broken, dirty, trembling before me. My breath, that had come so easily in the embrace of the wolf, fell short and ragged.

"H-how?" I stammered.

The crow squawked from a small round table.

I smiled, despite myself. "It's good to finally see you."

I pulled myself up to the table's top to properly greet my feathered savior perched on a hand mirror. He hopped off the mirror and called at me again. Unsure if I wanted to see just what had become of me, the crow called yet again. I drew a deep breath and lifted the mirror.

My eyes . . . .

Not *my* eyes. My eyes were green. The ones looking back at me were blue and brown. Mismatched. My face was bruised and battered, and the crows had carved a strange sigil in my forehead that was hot and tender to the touch. My hair, a matted mess caked with mud and blood and feathers . . . .

The feathers.

My armor covered me like a maiden knight, leaving only feet, hands, and head uncovered. I blinked. I did not recognize that girl looking back at me. Like I was seeing myself for the first time. In a way, it was exactly that. In ways that had nothing to do with the strangers' eyes doing the looking. The girl I was felt more of a stranger to me than the eyes. Who had I become? Who was this girl that was me, that was so determined to survive? She looked so worn, so broken. So ungodly resolute.

The crow pecked the table. Next to him sat a whole bowl full of eyes. They sloshed and bobbed when I slammed down the mirror. Could mine be–

I couldn't bring myself to finish that unspoken question. If pieces of me were there, then who else?

This time, my unspoken question answered itself. The small room was lit only by a single dusty window at the opposite end from me. A single beam of sunlight bore into the room and the crows outside began their chorus again. Troughs and shelves, trunks and jars, all of them, full of pieces. Parts. Women's arms, legs, hands. An eyeless head sat suspended in a jar with some unknown liquid. Her dark hair floated like earthy roots, growing the wrong direction. I wiped condensation from the jar face and I saw her. Truly saw her. And what's more, she saw me. Sorrowfully, I wiped at the jar some more. Her hair swayed in the agitated current. She wasn't eyeless, after all. Only halfway. And as I stared at her, I knew. Anguish seeped into me. Though it did not belong to me. Not entirely. It was the sort of pain that came from seeing yourself die and being helpless to do anything about it. I looked away, to spare her or, perhaps selfishly, myself.

It was impossible to tell how many women had been decimated here. An arm stuck out near my own, and for a reason I didn't understand, I held its hand. When my fingers wrapped around hers, I could feel her fear, her finality. My heart raced in my chest when I spotted a distinct freckle on her wrist. A tear from the blue eye silently ran down my face. I could hear them. All of them. And I just stood there, listening to the dead. Witnessing them. I understood then what needed to be done.

I ran out of the room. The crow took the lead. He squawked and fluttered at something coming.

"Get out of here, you filthy demon," the man bellowed. He stomped through the front door. "Tried to leave, did ye? Didn't get far." He pulled a brass key out from under his shirt, tied to his neck, and looked right at me.

What I saw was a buzzing shadow of a man. As if he was made of bees and all his parts forgot to come together. I squeezed my new eyes tightly shut, unsure if I could fully trust what I was seeing. I opened them, and he was whole. My insides turned at the sight of this familiar man standing before me. I recognized those dark eyes with no life or sincerity behind them. The moonlight shone off a glint of silver. Him, his weight, his shadow loomed over me, held me down. I tried so hard to only see the moon. But that night, I saw the devil too.

"You." Now it was my voice that changed into a shadow, a low-bellied growl. "You took my eyes. You did this to me." It wasn't just me who spoke. It was them. All of them. All the women he destroyed. We were unified in voice and strength. And my fear had left me for him.

"How did ye—?" The confusion on his face at the sight of my sight cleaned away his smile. "More magics. Who are you?"

"My name does not matter." I took a step forward. The floorboards creaked under my weight. And under his as he shifted backwards without taking a step.

"I am nothing and no one."

The key hung around his neck. My chain clanked.

"Just a girl in the wood."

Outside, the crows began a new chorus of judgment. They flocked around the cabin, darkening the windows.

"Far from castles and dreams."

The wolf joined me from the would-be crypt. Her brethren entered through a passage opened by the crows and joined my side.

"I run with the wolves."

A furious storm of feathers burst into the house. Crows circled all of us: him, the wolves, and me, entrapping us together in a murderous cage.

"I sing with the crows."

I took another step, my foot slowly rolling on broken window glass. And I did not flinch. I did not even feel it. The man looked at me with eyes full of terror.

I grinned. "I am the untamed daughter."

The animals attacked. Teeth and talon pulled him apart. Sinew snapped and bone cracked. He screamed, but only for a moment. When there was nothing left but bones, the crows and wolves quietly took their leave of the house. I knelt down beside the stain of blood on the floor. They'd left his eyes. And they were full of his silenced screaming. His agony would be eternal so long as those eyes, those dark, empty things, remained.

I plucked the key from that pile of gore and unlocked the shackle on my ankle. A lit oil lamp sat upon the mantle. I lifted the lamp to my eyes and gazed into the gentle dancing flame.

"I burn."

The lamp smashed on the floor, exploded into tendrils of flame in all directions. The fire swept through the house, eager to take it all to hell.

My crow met me by the gate and slid a hyacinth into my hair. I patted his head, and he flew for the trees. Above me, the stars began to bloom in the darkening sky, dancing around the waxing moon. With an easy smile on my face, I followed my crow back to the forest. Where I would wait for the day I find a scared girl with no eyes, who needs to find her strength to stand up.

IN THE TREES

ALEXIS L. CARROLL

"New planet G181MM Colonist log number two-two-three-uhhh..."

Dr. Siegfried Edmund stood with his back to the lab, staring at the outdoor view of the encampment. The stark white plastic domes looked pristine as ever against the blueberry hue of the foreign planet's terrain, the curious twin moons peeking just beyond. The terrain looked nearly identical to Earth's. Dirt, rocks, grass, mountains and forests. Yet everything was bathed in shades of blue. Dr. Edmund scratched his head, the white streak in his black braids had become much wider than when he first arrived on the planet. He could never remember what audio-journaling number he was on. It was such a minor detail to him, yet an essential part of their colonizing-prep mission.

"Log two-two-*seven*-three," came a reply after the whoosh of the automatic doors. Dr. Linus Pinkeen, in all his space treksuit glory, strutted towards his boss with a dying plant in one arm and a data screen in the other. He smirked as he approached. "You really ought to jot the number down on an erase board. Or, hell! This window you love staring out of so much."

Dr. Edmund shrugged with a sheepish grin. "Then what would you do, Dr. Pinkeen? What's that you've got there?"

Dr. Pinkeen sighed and handed the failed project over, then looked at his screen. "I just don't get it." He chewed on his lip, eyes roaming the data lists. "We grew our first batch with no problems. Now we can't keep an entire greenhouse alive? It's almost as if we're being sabotaged."

"Well, it was a bit different before." Dr. Edmund inspected the plant. "Our first garden, we started out slow and attentive. Now with the pressure to be successful colonizers, and get the ball rolling on human-portation to this planet, I think we've bitten off more than we can chew. We need more help, but damned if Control will give us another scientist."

Dr. Pinkeen scowled, fed up with the homebase's politics. He looked at the older scientist and admired how cheerful he still appeared, even holding a failed experiment. He tapped his finger against the back of the data screen. An idea popped forefront in his mind. They had discussed it before, but Dr. Edmund had said no. Dr. Pinkeen hoped that approaching the subject again would be more fruitful than their dying greenhouse. "You know, my second major was engineering. It's worth a shot for us to try and build extra help. Just a small AI, Seig. Please?"

They really did not have the time to fiddle around with AI, but Dr. Pinkeen was intelligent enough to pull it off, and Dr. Edmund knew this. If they put their minds together, and kept it a small project, there wouldn't be any harm in it. "Hm . . . Alright, but if it takes longer than two weeks we have to scrap the idea and focus solely on converting plant life here on G181MM. We can only work on it off the clock and with scrap technology laying around."

"You won't regret this." Dr. Pinkeen clenched his fist, face alight with excitement. He leaned forward and landed a kiss on Dr. Edmund's cheek. "Now, let's get to dinner. I've got a bottle of wine aerating already."

THE DEADLINE DR. EDMUND had set for the AI project was close at hand, and try as they might, creating a useful robot from scraps became more fleeting every day. Dr. Pinkeen sat outside eating a freeze-dried fruit of which he could no longer tell the kind of, in the safety of their encampment, his data screen in his lap. With a sad sigh, he shook his head at the readings. The tech was just too old for what he wanted it to do. He pushed the red call button on his treksuit sleeve.

Dr. Edmund's electronic voice came through the speaker of his suit. "Dr. Pinkeen? Is everything alright?"

"Yes, sir. I was wondering if I could go scouting for a bit, to clear my head, get more soil samples. If that's alright with you?" Dr. Pinkeen awaited the answer, but packed away his things anyway.

"Of course. That sounds like a great idea. Enjoy your walk, doctor." The comm buzzed, signaling the end of their connection.

It felt good to get out, to explore. Thirteen months stationed on the blue planet and Dr. Pinkeen still found new things every time he ventured out. That day he planned on going farther than he ever had before. The fuzzy tingle of the force field let him know he was stepping beyond their security barrier. Turning left, he decided to hike one of the smaller cerulean mountains. As he ascended, his treksuit beeped six times, an alert that O_2 in the area was too low for humans. A problem they were trying to fix. At the top, Dr. Pinkeen was out of breath but felt marvelous, his endorphins high.

The view was stunning.

To his left, more of the deep blue mountains. To his right, a valley vibrant in shades similar to an ocean. The planet's natural plant life swayed in a gentle breeze, mimicking waves. Ahead, the unexplored Azure Forest with tall, twisted trees that maintained its thick wall. It called to him with an unspoken voice so sweet, so strong. After a steep climb down, he breached the border. A pause held him at its mercy, a limbo between turning back in fear or unbridled excitement at exploring the unknown. One foot inside and excitement won out.

A half hour's trek found Dr. Pinkeen deep within the forest, under a canopy of multi-hued blues, and strange bird-like whistles but no tail feather nor furry creature to be seen. A glade with a large, black rock in its center came into focus and called to him.

"A meteor?" Dr. Pinkeen cried out, giddy at the prospect of something new to study.

Crossing the glade's perimeter, his treksuit went haywire in alert. He stopped, alarmed, and scanned the area. Nothing came back. He tapped the screen and watched it go blank. As unusual as that was, he decided to ignore the suit's warning, and now lack of tech, to get closer to the meteor. Some things were worth the risk.

The onyx color stood out from the blue vegetation that threatened to engulf it, giving the rock an odd shape. Like an extremely large human lying on its side. "A sleeping giant," Dr. Pinkeen marveled. "Let's get some pictures and a sample, shall we?" It felt less lonely on the planet when he talked to objects, even though they never talked back. He scraped some of the meteor into a sample tube, then pulled out his data screen for photos. Whatever had made his suit go crazy, made his data screen even worse. Every photo came out overexposed, if it came out at all. He sighed. A rustling sound drew his attention.

Coming around the meteor, Dr. Pinkeen stopped, mouth agape. Before him stood the most beautiful indigo tree he had ever seen. It was twice as wide as he, with long, swooping branches that housed vibrant, neon blue flowers. A gentle hum came from the tree, carried on the wind. The closer he got, the stronger the hum became. It was a strange, disjointed melody.

His hand shook as he placed it against the dark blue trunk. The tree shuddered, loosening flowers that fell all around like snow. The glint of something metallic hiding under the bark seemingly the source. He peeled back the protective layer, revealing two perfect rectangles in the base. "Is this a port?!" He stumbled back, looking around the field. Were they not alone after all? Before they had set up the encampment, Control had done a thorough scan. There was no other human life on the planet. At least, that was what he was told.

Curiosity overtook him. He had to know what this port was, why it fit his technology if they were the first and only people there. He should report back to Dr. Edmund right away and wait for orders, wait for him to be present during the inspection. He withdrew the connector to his data screen from his utility pack, twisted it around his palm, then squared his shoulders. He had to know *now*.

He half-expected nothing to happen, but was surprised

when the battery icon lit up and went from half-charged to full in an instant. Files on the screen started opening and closing, scrolling, and flying around. The humming of the tree got louder. The flowers and the trunk's flesh beneath the bark began to glow and pulsate. Dr. Pinkeen stood transfixed by the sight. His treksuit started beeping again, warning him that the data screen in his hands was getting so hot it was near melting, even though it was designed to withstand extreme temperatures. The tree shook violently.

PZZZT.

Everything stopped. The data screen. The foliage's neon glow. The humming.

Dr. Pinkeen hadn't realized he was holding his breath until he gasped in the filtered air of his suit. A tremble ran through him as he looked up at the great tree. "Dr. Edmund is never going to believe this," he whistled. The data screen dinged, the noise it made after a restart, and he looked down. His eyes widened. "And he'll never believe this either."

) ▶ ● ◉ ◀ ((

THE TALE of the indigo glowing tree was less far fetched after Dr. Pinkeen showed Dr. Edmund an alien folder the tree installed on his data screen along with the meteor sample. Two weeks had passed before they could decipher enough of the information to deem its worth. "This is the most ingenious work I have ever seen," Dr. Pinkeen said. "You realize what this means?"

Dr. Edmund laughed. "Dr. Pinkeen, we can make your robot. This is exactly the kind of technology we've been missing. And maybe, we can finally colonize this planet.

Together." He wrapped his hand around the younger scientist's and smiled. Dr. Pinkeen's complexion paled and he swayed in Dr. Edmund's arms. "Are you okay?"

"I'm fine," Dr. Pinkeen replied, though a rough cough overtook him and he trembled as he covered his mouth. Dr. Edmund patted his back until the fit receded. When his throat no longer felt clogged, Dr. Pinkeen moved his hand away and gasped when he saw blood in his palm. "Or maybe I'm . . . not fine."

Although Dr. Pinkeen dying from severe radiation poisoning was tragic, it *was* his own fault for ignoring the warnings on their highly accurate treksuits. Dr. Kaine Joan couldn't help feeling giddy at having the opportunity to work with her idol, Dr. Edmund. On the legendary planet, G181MM, no less. The fact that he had not met her at the shuttle bay only added to the anticipation of their meeting. She passed rooms of various environments and plants. Soon those would be hers to work in and grow things. Pride beamed out of her when she thought of the miracles she would create there. The glass doors to the main lab whooshed open and with a deep breath to steady herself, Dr. Joan stepped inside, searching out Dr. Edmund with a sweeping gaze. She found him with a young man and waited to be acknowledged.

Five minutes passed.

He never looked up. He did not seem to have noticed her presence at all. That irritated her. Wasn't he expecting her, maybe even excited to meet a top Control scientist? With a shake of her shoulders to rid herself of the negative thoughts, and boost her confidence, Dr. Joan cleared her throat as loud as she could. "Dr. Edmund? I've arrived safely," she called over.

Both Dr. Edmund and the young man looked over at her, the doctor with a soldering tool in one hand and magnifying tech goggles over his eyes. The young man's blue eyes glowed unnaturally. "Oh, so you have!" He motioned for her to join them. When she did, he grabbed her hand and shook it, then placed it into the young man's hand. "This is Ivon. Ivon, this is . . . I'm sorry, dear, I'm afraid I forgot the briefing. What was your name and line of work?"

Stunned that her idol was a bumbling, forgetful man rather than the intelligent, award-winning scientist of renown, Dr. Joan haphazardly shook Ivon's hand. She noticed it was cold and felt devoid of texture like normal skin. "It's Joan. Dr. Kaine Joan. And I am a top botanist sent from Control. This . . . is amazing. Ivon, is it? The AI that you built with Dr. Pinkeen?" She could not believe how lifelike it seemed. Despite being amazed, she pulled her hand away and wiped it on her treksuit. Something about it put her on edge.

"Oh, a botanist again! Great! We were fixing a hole in the greenhouse when Ivon had a spill." He pointed to the robot's leg. Its silicone flesh was torn, internal hardware exposed. Dr. Edmund sighed. "Yes, Dr. Pinkeen was . . . well . . . a dear friend, to say the least. He will be sorely missed . . . I'm sorry." He turned away from her, rubbing at his eye with his shoulder as he did.

Dr. Joan reached out, giving him a pat that felt too personal, too awkward. "I'm sorry for your loss, sir. But I'm here now. We'll get this mission back on track. I'll even help fix this thing up for you."

"Thank you, Dr. Joan. I just know you'll be happy here." Dr. Edmund smiled through his tears. "Ivon is the last thing Dr. Pinkeen and I worked on together. He's nothing short of a miracle."

HAPPY WAS the farthest thing Dr. Joan felt after three months on planet with Dr. Edmund and his prized possession, Ivon. The AI could do no wrong in his eyes, yet it made more work for Dr. Joan because of how curious and clumsy the thing was. One day it had switched the soils she was working with. Took her hours to realize why the pH balance was off. Another time, it spilled a brand-new batch of pesticides she had devoted the better part of two weeks perfecting. Though she had no way to prove any of those instances. And the questions. It asked. So. Many. Questions.

As a bonding tool, Dr. Joan had instigated another AI build with Dr. Edmund, hoping to be rid of Ivon while at the same time winning over her superior. It failed miserably. He wept on and off during the process, often having to leave her to work on her own. And the files Dr. Pinkeen had used for Ivon's intelligence were mysteriously corrupt. Now she was stuck with two AI robots; one that was too childlike and the other braindead in comparison. She only used AI-II to move heavy things around. That's about all it was good for. She really hated robots, yet those two followed her around like pets.

Pain drew Dr. Joan out of a really difficult text she was reading. AI-II dropped a box on her foot. "Grrr! You blasted piece of junk!" She slammed her fist on the desk.

The action startled Ivon, who had been misting plants,

and it made a beeline to her. "Do you need medical assistance?" Its face was so human-like in concern, it would have been convincing if not for its glowing eyes.

"No, you idiot! I'm fine!" She slammed her fist again, this time knocking the data screen around. This was not what she had signed up for when she agreed to take over the colonization of the planet. When she reached for her data screen, the text had changed and she stared at malware disguised as a website ad for cheap plants. She rubbed her temples, frustrated. Before she closed the website, a thought struck her. She side-eyed the smarter of the two robots. It was a devious thought, utterly selfish of her.

Later that night, by the dim light of two moons, she snuck into the main lab and turned on the AI-dock with a swipe of her key card. Both robots were powered down, recharging. She withdrew her personal data stick and tapped it to the screen. It lit up right away then made distressed beeps as the screen went fuzzy and green. An angry, pixelated face appeared and she typed in the code to send it into Ivon's hardware. Noise outside of the lab startled her and she quickly shut the screen off. Peeking through the glass door, Dr. Joan didn't see anything or anyone in the hall, but she didn't want to chance being caught. She'd see the damage in the morning.

) ☽ ● ◖Ⓥ◗ ● ☾ (

"Wake up! Wake up, you stupid bot!" Dr. Joan urged AI-II, a tremble in her hands as she scanned her key card.

Upon her return in the morning, Ivon was much worse than she had anticipated. Black soot stained the sides of its neck and ears, a clear sign of short circuiting. If Dr. Edmund saw it like that, he would know she messed with it since the other robot was fine. AI-II powered up and smiled, then looked at its brother expectantly.

"Don't just sit there, get up! We have to dispose of this," Dr. Joan hissed, motioning to Ivon.

Together they dismantled and packed Ivon into a box, then Dr. Joan sent AI-II with instructions to go out farther than any of them had ever been, determined to never have Dr. Edmund find the evidence. She watched until AI-II was out of sight, over the cerulean mountains, nerves twisting in her gut.

Hours passed before Dr. Edmund came into Dr. Joan's lab, a joyous smile on his face, touching each plant on his way to her, seeming none the wiser to the devious happenings. "Dr. Joan! Good afternoon. How is your research going?"

Dr. Joan felt feverish, sweat moistening her pits. "Good, I suppose."

"Why, you don't look well, Dr. Joan," Dr. Edmund stood beside her, alarmed. He grabbed her hand. "And your hands are clammy. Are you getting sick? Goodness, we can't have that happening. We must get Ivon to scan you. Nip this in the bud. Where is he?"

Dr. Joan snatched her hand away. "It's gone. Ivon went on a scouting mission for me. Whenever it gets back, I'll have it scan me. I am sure I'm fine, maybe just overworked. Nothing a nap can't fix." She laughed, hoping it didn't sound suspicious. She had forgotten what a terrible liar she was.

"Well, alright then. Once he is back, get scanned. That is an order," Dr. Edmund's eyes glossed over, restrained tears in the waterline. "I can't lose another person I care about. Linus had said he was fine, too . . ."

Her heart quickened and her stomach soured. He cared about her? It was too late to regret her transgressions, too late to fix what she had done. "I promise, I'll take care of myself," she said softly, moving her hand back into Dr. Edmund's. Maybe her plan to bring them closer would work after all.

) ◗ ● ◖ ● ◖ (

AI-II DID NOT KNOW how far any of the humans had gone. The information Dr. Joan uploaded to his navigation went fuzzy just inside the Azure Forest. Still, he trekked on until he came to a clearing with a large meteor. There were no signs of life-forms on his radar, but there was an electrical current nearby that seemed to call to him. AI-II took his broken brother to the source of the electrical scan and discovered a tree hidden behind the meteor. He put Ivon back together, though he had no tools to connect the pieces and his master had said to dispose of him. It was difficult to disobey a direct order, but when he calculated the chances of Ivon surviving as broken as he was, it satisfied his objective enough. Behind Ivon, the tree shimmered, shaking flowers free of its branches. A charging port that fit their needs appeared. When AI-II connected Ivon to the glowing indigo tree, a spark came out and singed his plastic cheek, tickling the circuits. His brother would be okay, he just knew it. AI-II left, humming a song he hadn't seen in his memory bank before.

)◗●◍◖◖(

"WHAT THE BLOODY HECK IS THIS?!"

"What the bloody heck is WHAT?!"

"THIS!" A being no taller than an Earth crow screamed. It jumped up and down next to the broken robot's body, tiny hands rolled into fists. The light from full twin moons made his powder blue skin glimmer, though his face threatened to turn violent purple with rage. Iridescent wings flitted erratically. "I told you those human scums would trash our beloved planet! You said they couldn't pass the sleeping giant's poison. Look at this! RUBBISH!"

The other fairy sighed and set down his basket full of the neon blue flowers to inspect the humans' rubbish. He circled the thing, tapping his spindly finger against his face. He was more of a cyan color than the other. "And I told *you* not to go messing with their camp. That it would only lead them back to us." With a kick, he jostled its broken arm, and scanned over the too-real texture of its fake skin. His navy blue brows knitted together. "Something's not right about this robot. This is too similar to our tech."

"I TOLD YOU!" yelled his companion. "We must tell the Queen about this! She will be furious! And then those humans will pay." His grin was wicked, sharp pointy teeth gleaming. He was a bloodthirsty one, no doubt.

The other small being nodded in agreement. "Let's bring it back to the palace. I'm sure she'll want to see what they have been doing." He knocked on the thing's closed eyes. The two unplugged it, the charging port disappeared, and they sprinkled a shimmering stardust on top of it. The robot rose into the air, lighter than a feather, and was guided deeper into the forest by the two fairies.

)🌙●◍◖◖(

A SHARP SLAP to the face startled Dr. Joan awake. Eyes blurry, she couldn't make out the numbers on her alarm clock. Rubbing the sleep away, she soon realized it was because it no longer showed numbers but instead displayed strange symbols. A small sting on her cheek reminded her why she had awoken. Who slapped her? Angry whispering tickled her ear, a faint buzzing sound.

Standing on her pillow was a tiny, humanoid alien with four arms and two sets of gossamer wings. Its body was a pale blue, and on its head wild, curly dark blue hair with black-as-pitch stubby horns protruding outwards. Its bug-like eyes were wide and shiny black as it shook all four of its fists at her. She tried to scream, but the creature blew a dark powder right into her face. Every muscle in her being froze.

A second creature fluttered down from the shadows, with a large scythe and stone-cold face. The creature lifted its arms, the moons' light flashing on the scythe as it came swinging toward her.

Crimson red splattered the walls.

"Hey! What should we do with the other scumbag?"

The deathbringer rubbed its chin as it kicked the head down to the floor with a splat. "Her Majesty watched the robot's playback. She said the male human was good natured and wished to have him for her collection."

With a nod, the troublemaker clasped two hands together while a third hand pulled out the bag of floating stardust.

"FATHER. Awaken, Father. Our captors have ensured no harm has come to you. I have scanned you and found it to be true."

Dr. Edmund opened heavy eyes, struggling through an unusual grogginess. It took a while to adjust, it was much darker than normal. He realized he was not in the bright, white sanctity of their Control lab. He could not remember anything, only going to bed concerned about his partner Dr. Joan. Yet he recognized the voice that awoke him. "Ivon?"

"Yes, Father. It is I, your beloved son, Ivon. I have missed you." The AI robot smiled, a new twinkle to his neon blue eyes, seeming even more human-like than before. He reached out and helped Dr. Edmund stand. "It is so nice to have you home with me."

"Home? But where are we? We are not in the lab. Where is Dr. Joan? Is she okay?"

"No, not the lab. Our true home. Where I belong, where my technology comes from. We are in the land of the fairies," Ivon explained simply. "And here we can be together. Forever. The fairies have taken care of Dr. Joan. She was not a nice woman."

"What do you mean 'was not'?" Dr. Edmund looked around at the room they were in. It resembled one of those small apartments from Earth he had seen in history screens, with relics such as a stove, a couch, a table and matching chairs. The hairs on the back of Dr. Edmund's neck prickled. "Ivon, did you say fairies?" When he looked up, hundreds of small, blue faces stared down at him. He shook in fear.

Ivon's arms wrapped around him.

"Do not worry, Father. The Queen knows you are a just

human and has agreed to keep us in her collection. Forever. And you'll build more of me. Brothers and sisters."

His eyes met with a pair of large luminescent ones, a crown of neon blue flowers around her head, four periwinkle horns twirling outwards. She stood in the center of the crowd behind the glass roof, a faint hint of a smile on her lips. The Fairy Queen turned away, taking with her the onlookers.

As they left, the light of the exhibits turned off one by one until the zoo was lit only by the twin moons high above.

THE GIRL WHO WASN'T FEAR

AMANDA STOCKTON

Doom upon all the world, a whisper steeled with the weight of violence with the end of everything Lyra knew or loved.

It used to be that she could sit upon that hill and watch the torchlights of the solstice marchers as they sang their sacred songs and rang the bells of spirit blessing. Lyra would run away, escape to the hill to be alone, where she could hide and no one except Niriam, the town herbalist, knew where she was.

Fireflowers grew under the moon in the warmer months, painting the hill in a glowing pink aura. Now there was only smoke. A painfully endless rising that painted the moon red until it choked out completely, bathing the world in a blanket of darkness. But the sun, too, would rise. The promise of a future never to be seen by her people. It was only Lyra now. Just her and that smoke. And it was in her hair, on her skin. Goddess help her, she could feel it wafting through her bones.

The smoke kept the southern sky black even as the sun broke away the night. She stood up from the damp earth, not caring about the mud clinging to the knees of her blue dress. Her hands had finally stopped shaking. Sometime during the night, they'd become stranger's hands, crusted in her mother's blood, unfamiliar . . . grisly. Even as the moment replayed in her head, she couldn't remember when her hands had changed. When they'd failed to stop the life from pouring out of her mother? When they clung to her after her heart stopped beating? Her fingers curled, grasping onto the only thing she had left of family.

There were no more tears to shed. She'd cried them all out during the night, and her eyes burned with the leftover fury of her despair. The rest of her, however, had numbed. The cold twist in her chest subsided. She told herself the worst part was over. But she was still on that hill. She was still alive and now, alone. The time for fear had ended and, in her mind, there was only one option left to her.

Twice Lyra had counted the number of footsteps between Niriam's herbary and the top of her hill. Three hundred and forty-seven steps. Three hundred and forty-seven chances to turn around, spare herself the sight. Lyra, however, had no intention of cowering. She needed to go.

The Forgotten was where all dead things go, even places, entire cities and towns like Lyra's Omareen. The Pilgrims saw sin in their land; thought it just, in the eyes of their god, to burn it down—burn the people with it. But unlike a corpse, when a place dies, it becomes something else. Twisted by the blood soaked into its earth and the screams that echoed against its still-smoldering bones.

"This is not my home," she told herself. And she was right; it was hell. So, when her feet kicked some unmentionable gore on the ground, she didn't scream. Because those were not her people. Those were hell's commodities.

Three hundred and forty-seven steps came and went.

But the herbary with its brightly colored eaves and window shutters had been reduced to little more than cinder and ash. She'd expected it. The fire raged all night, lit the sky with its violent purification. And the screams . . . the screams were one thing. It was the silence that fell after the screaming that haunted her.

Knowing the truth and seeing it were not the same thing. As Lyra observed the destruction of the shop her mother had worked in for a lifetime, an icy wave of grief washed over her.

"Lyra! Up the hill. Go, now." A hand clutched onto Lyra's arm. Niriam's once soft features had gone glowing red, pocked by angry weeping wounds. Her wild white curls had been shaved. The mark of the Pilgrims—a wreath of flames encircling three pillars—burned as a brand on Niriam's forehead. Her grip on Lyra's arm sizzled her skin.

"Let me go!" Lyra stumbled, fell backwards. It wasn't Niriam, not really. The thing didn't even have legs. It was all fire and distorted, stolen memory.

"Go. Lyra. The hill. The hill." The spectre's features dulled. Its burning edges softened and even the details of its face that made it so distinctly Niriam, flattened like a poorly rendered caricature. She muttered about herbs and drifted around the shop, maneuvering around phantom furniture.

"I'm sorry," Lyra whispered. Even though she knew it wasn't Niriam, it was made from her memories, from pieces of her that stained this place. Haunted it.

A spectre wasn't a spirit, not really. It was a scar. An open wound between body and earth, between soul and bone. This spectre was energy bleeding from between the Forgotten and Omareen, feeding on the memories that saturated the grounds.

"Oh! Lyra," the spectre called out. "Now, take these tinctures to your mother." It approached and stopped suddenly, hitting a wall of realization. "Oh–I . . . What's happened–I . . ."

Lyra watched helplessly as the spectre looped back to fear. It lunged at her again, all fire and pain. Lyra dodged out of the spectre's reach and stepped back beyond the borders of the herbary. It came up to and passed the foundation line and continued to close the gap between them.

"Shit." Lyra stepped backwards. It was worse than she thought. Feeding off of Niriam's energy, the spectre should have been confined to the property lines. But it was not a typical spectre. There had been too much fear here. Too much violence. It caused a fracture expanding outward, allowing the creature to move along the imperceptible cracks, however far they reached.

"They're coming. The Pilgrims." The spectre spoke with Niriam's voice, her memories, her inflections. It spoke with Niriam's fear. "With one of their own on the throne, no one is safe. No one is–"

Lyra darted around the wandering creature and into the ashes of the herbary.

The spectre turned to follow, but Niriam's orange eyes rattled around its ethereal head, looking desperately for the building that wasn't there. "Where—why—I . . ." it stammered, unable to stitch together a complete thought. And instead screamed, "They're here! The Pilgrims will take us all!" The spectre screeched through a ragged throat and hacked up black bile from its core. "Sinner! The gates of Tesperoth await you."

It raised an accusatory finger at Lyra and screeched again. The sound was so utterly devastating, Lyra couldn't decide if she should cover her ears or collapse to her knees and scream with it.

The spectre came for her again. Its orange glow burnt darker. A hellfire of reckoning, calling out holy wrath by the names of dead gods.

On her knees, Lyra struggled, desperately digging for anything that could help fend off the creature. Her hand tore against something sharp. She pulled the broken jar from its would-be grave and exhaled sharply when she found it still held a generous amount of black salt. With her bloodied hand, Lyra gripped a handful of ash, added it to the jar, and ran.

The spectre glared at the jar and snarled. "Sin. Sin. You will hang from the third pillar in the fires of His eye, just like your whore mother."

The black salt wouldn't destroy the spectre. But it would contain it. And with the jar in her hands, the spectre slowed its pursuit of her. More black sap wept from its mouth, drooling over its want of her. Over its engrained purpose set upon it by the Pilgrims who created it with their cruelty.

"Little girls." Its words came out disjointed and wet. "Little sinful girls make a hearty feast for crows."

Lyra ignored the beast's words but kept herself aimed at it, sure to keep the jar secure while she did. One hand was slick with blood and the other with sweat. As if in response to the fear that gripped her heart, a smile twisted on the spectre's mouth. It raised its nose at her, sniffed the air. The beast's smile cut wide across its face, opened like a sack of burning flesh. Two skeletal hands wedged their way out of the spectre's mouth.

The spectre screamed and gargled and spit up more black bile around the thing that crawled out of it.

Lyra dropped the jar.

Out from the depths of the spectre climbed a half-charred, half-bone bane plague. It slapped to the ground, a slippery newborn abysmal demon chosen especially for Lyra.

Its joints cracked and popped into whatever place as it oriented itself into a somewhat human-looking figure. But it was all wrong. Like something trying to look human without ever having seen one. Its fleshy parts bled black sap, bones rattled like wind chimes. Misshapen and lopsided, the bane plague looked as though all its parts belonged to different people: A pile of burnt corpses turned inside out, hastily strewn together into one nightmare of a beast.

She'd never seen a bane plague. Truth be told, Lyra hadn't been entirely sure they were real. Not until the moment one was spat out before her. She collected herself. The salt. The jar was shattered at her feet. Her line around the foundations incomplete.

The bane plague twisted its head around and found Lyra grasping handfuls of salt with her bare hands. She whimpered as it burrowed in her wounded palm. But she had to finish her task before the creature realized what she was doing. And even then, Lyra had no idea if it would still work.

Lyra poured the salt from her hands, working along the building's border. The bane plague clacked and rattled and chomped. Wobbling like a fawn on unsure legs. Its head tilted too far. Sinew snapped. Slack jawed, a pustule-pink tongue rolled out of its mouth. Thrup, its tongue whipped back into its rotating jaw that dripped with drool in long, spidery tendrils. The beast's crooked spine snapped into place with two quick jerks of its shoulders.

The bane plague turned its misaligned eyes to Lyra. She made the mistake of looking at them. Seeing them. Recognizing them. That's what that stupid smile on the spectre's face was about. Those eyes had comforted Lyra through storms and sleepless nights. Facing what was in the head of that creature, with its melted flesh and putrid bone, Lyra lost the strength in her arms. They fell limp at her sides. Of all the things she both needed–and not needed–it was to look into her mother's eyes.

For a moment, Lyra forgot to breathe. And then time caught up with her, and breath came fast and shallow. She screamed and charged at the demon. Too easily did the monster swoop her up by the throat. It looked at her with her mother's eyes as she turned a precarious shade of blue.

Then Lyra was flying through the air. Why the bane plague chose to throw her instead of just biting off her head, Lyra didn't particularly care. She met the ground with a rolling pain, from this shoulder to that one, and skid to a stop.

Lyra's arms shook under her weight as she tried to push herself up. They gave out, sending her collapsing back into the dirt. Her ragged breath stirred the dust. Hands clutched at the earth. When she looked for the bane plague, she found it trapped behind the salt. She knew the circle had been incomplete, and the bane plague would know it too. But instead, it wanted to prove a point. More than that, it wanted to show just how terrified she should be.

The bane plague pushed against the invisible barrier with bony fingers. At first it was slow, difficult movements capped with weeping blisters bubbling as the bane plague pressed against its cage. Then it decided to put in just a little bit of effort. The barrier sparked. The bane plague's hands sizzled and smoked. Putrid flesh melted from blighted bone and, still, it pushed its way into the salt barrier. When it called out, it wasn't in pain or distress. The sound it made ran a chill down Lyra's spine. Because it wasn't just laughter, and it wasn't just pride. It was knowledge of the deepest, darkest points of shame and misery Lyra had ever felt. And it made that noise while it looked at her with her mother's eyes and made an example of how little power Lyra had.

Instead of running back and fighting, Lyra clambered to her feet to flee. Though she didn't get far, the sounds of the bane plague's jest still rang in her ears. Her legs trembled and her chest heaved. She was just a little girl. Thirteen was too young to live as much life as she had in one day. But she knew it wasn't over. The bane plague would hunt her for as long as it took in order to drag her through the coals. She had to fight. But how?

"From Earth, Nixus plucked her gifts of armor: a pillar of salt and crown made of iron." *Iron.* Lyra raced towards the blacksmith's shop. Burnt down or not, a surplus of iron would be left in the rubble. And the faster she got there, the more time she would have to dig through the debris.

A gentle clang of iron against iron echoed along the path Lyra ran. She slowed, stopped. Crept the rest of the way to the blacksmith's with quiet steps and bated breath. She heard it before she saw it: fire crackling and something heavy being dragged behind stomping boots.

Lyra crouched behind the debris of a collapsed stable near the blacksmith's shop. Through the tangled mess of burnt and broken beams, Lyra spotted a pair of large black boots buckled up to the thick knees of a man, dragging a ragged body through the gravel behind him. He tossed it on the fire, clapped the filth from his hands, and rolled up the sleeves of his black linen shirt. Around his neck, hanging under a long blond beard, a silver medallion: a wreath of flame around three pillars. A Pilgrim, there to clean up after he and his brethren destroyed Omareen. There to burn the rest of the bodies.

Lyra's head fell. The weight of another monster in her midst pulled on her faith. When she wanted to turn heel and run, when she questioned why she ever came down from her hill, she shook her head in reply. "No more running," she told her lingering fears. "Today, I am done running."

Lyra stood to her fullest height, abandoning her hiding place to face the Pilgrim. He was just a man in monster's clothing.

He stared down at her from a height of nearly double Lyra's as though she were a strange apparition. With no weapon at his hip, it was clear he'd not been expecting any interruptions, let alone a survivor. Least of all a fight.

"Well, well," the Pilgrim said with a dark raspy voice. "Looks like we've got ourselves a little lost rabbit."

Lyra's eyes pinned to the man, unyielding. She walked out from behind the debris. A challenge or a surrender, she left it up to the Pilgrim to decide how he wished to interpret her actions.

"Where have you been hiding, little rabbit girl?" He clicked his tongue, brought a cigarette to his lips. An insidious smile cracked across his face before taking a long drag.

Small and shaking in her dress, Lyra straightened her back, sure to keep her glare square on the Pilgrim. A paste of blood and ash and salt and earth caked her wounded hand. She turned it away from view. But a principle bleed betrayed her instead. Her body tensed, feeling the wet drip down her legs.

"Not girl then." The Pilgrim slowly reached for something sitting amongst the outer embers of the pyre. His eyes flicked from the blood running down her leg up to her face. His breath, calculated. "Shame, that. A girl might have had a chance for redemption. Now you're just another Omarion whore." He knew, just as well as Lyra, her entrance to womanhood was also one into power.

The Pilgrim's fingers wrapped around an iron. Lyra's wrapped through the air, twisting and calling upon something from elsewhere.

"You're going to hold really, very still now, little rabbit."

"Do you know what I think?" Lyra asked. "I think you're afraid of a little menstrual blood."

His lip curled, his knuckles turned white on the branding iron, bright orange and angry, ready for her flesh. To condemn her. To save her immortal soul.

Black smoke appeared around Lyra's hands. A new sensation tingled in her veins. She found it so naturally, no different from breathing. The smoke faded between there and that other place. In and out of perception, between her fingers, up her arms. Power manifested differently in every Omarion. Spawned in her first bleed as a woman, Lyra's power was born on the heels of disaster. And so disaster would be what she wrought.

The Pilgrim's solemn expression hardened, his sneer creased into a brutish smile, all tooth and beard. "Here little rabbit, I've got something for you to nibble."

Lyra's power flowed to her shoulders, a warm scarf around her neck.

The Pilgrim ran at her, branding iron at the ready.

The smoke turned inward, filling Lyra through her nostrils and between gritted teeth. Her sight clouded before black tears fell down her cheeks.

"Witch! You will hang from the thir—"

"The third pillar, yes. So I've been told."

Just as the hot iron made for Lyra's face, she pushed her hands together, formed a ball of smoke, and yanked them apart.

The iron fell. It swung through the cloud of smoke and hit the earth where she'd once stood.

"Beast!" he called. "Coward!"

Lyra materialized behind the man. With her wounded hand, she shoved him in the back, leaving part of herself on his shirt. Barely affected by her force, the Pilgrim twisted around and backhanded Lyra across the face.

She landed on her backside and kicked her feet, pushing herself away from him.

"Pageantry tricks won't save you, rabbit." With little effort the Pilgrim closed the gap. He clicked his tongue again. Lifted the iron. "May the pillars reap justice."

Before he could swing, the bane plague smashed into him. Together, they crashed through the barely standing wall of Piotr's tavern.

"Worked better than I expected," Lyra muttered. She got up and called the power again.

Another opportunity for her to run away, let those two monsters destroy one another. But Lyra had other plans.

A breath filled her lungs, found a place where her fear still lived, and wrapped around it. Then she was off, following the trail of destruction the bane plague and the Pilgrim left in their wake.

When Lyra caught up to them, the demon was snapping its jaw at the Pilgrim in a tight, struggling embrace. Lyra waited to see if it would sink its grotesque teeth into the Pilgrim's face when the toe of her boot hit the branding iron.

Lyra approached the bane plague from behind,

branding iron tight in her grip. She took her time, in no rush to save the Pilgrim or stop their fight. Its wet jaw snapped at the Pilgrim's face and throat like a rabid dog. The man barely held it off as he tore at its sinew, snapping the demon's connective tissue. Buying himself precious seconds to find another point of attack before it put itself back together again.

Lyra swung the iron as hard as she could into the bane plague's dripping skull. It paused. Looked at the Pilgrim as though he had been the offending party. Lyra pulled the iron back and swung again. It smashed through the blighted bone and stuck.

"Not the head, then." Lyra's attack only managed to anger it further.

The bane plague tossed the Pilgrim, but not before snapping his arm like a chicken's neck. The man screamed out in pain, but the howling of the bane plague drowned out everything else.

It turned back to Lyra. Her mother's eyes rolled around in its head, clanking around in sockets too large. It reached for the iron still stuck in its skull and yanked it out. She thought it might hit her. But they both knew it didn't need a weapon. It *was* the weapon.

Black smoke rushed up her arms. She held them up defensively. Lyra looked into her mother's eyes. It should have broken her. Made her weak. Made her scream out in agony and rage—but it didn't. If there was some piece of her mother trapped within that monster, Lyra would destroy that prison.

The breath she held around that ball of fear released in a war cry so loud it rivaled that of the spectre. Everything Lyra kept inside–every ounce of pain and loneliness and fear–exploded out of her. A dark rage of smoke wrapped itself around the bane plague. Into it. Between its dripping flesh and festered bone. And still she didn't stop screaming. The smoke started to pull the bane plague apart. Pulled at its limbs, cracked its bones, expanding from the inside of the demon, growing out of it like wild roots.

The bane plague shook and screamed back at Lyra, but it couldn't find the same pitch. So instead, it struck her. With a skeletal hand to the face, Lyra was back down on the ground. Blood poured from her nose and she spit out what hadn't drained down her throat.

While the bane plague fought to escape the smoke, Lyra wiped her nose and thighs with her fingers. Using her own blood like ink, she scrawled runes up her arms. The surrounding smoke turned red, and within it, a dozen iron knives manifested. She threw her hands forward, and the knives flew at the creature. They penetrated their mark and pushed it back.

Lyra retrieved the branding iron and swung it around in her grip.

The bane plague tore at the knives stuck in its body, choking on its own juices. It freed one blade and threw it at Lyra. Sliced her shoulder, dying her dress more scarlet than blue.

She didn't slow down. She didn't stop. She couldn't. One moment's hesitation and the creature would overtake her.

Lyra swung the iron at its core. It shuddered. She swung again. It screamed. The third swing cracked open the bane plague's chest. And the fourth struck it right in the heart. It burst. A black scourge splattered across Lyra's face, her hands, her chest.

The bane plague twitched and clattered. Its eyes flicked between Lyra and the iron stuck in its chest. With futile gestures of its lingering hunger, the demon clicked its teeth and curled its trembling fingers toward Lyra.

Looking into her mother's eyes, one last time, Lyra pulled the iron free.

The bane plague shuddered and its jaw opened wide, as it turned its head to the sky. Lyra's black smoke enveloped the demon and flowed into its gaping maw.

A final rasp escaped the monster's jaws and its eyes faded to a white nothingness. The demon's corpse steamed into a puddle of sticky black tar. In the middle of which, sparkled a faint glimmer of silver.

Applause. Clapping of one hand against a leg. The Pilgrim reappeared, one arm dangling, broken, at his side. He spat a swill of mucus and blood. And then, without terms of endearment, he was after her.

Lyra dropped to the ground. Grasped the weapon in the muck at her feet. The Pilgrim froze. A dumbfounded look spread across his face. He spat again. Choked on his own blood that painted his lips a brilliant crimson red. The demon dagger, a silver-white blade of twisted steal with a grip of black blighted bone, pierced right into the Pilgrim's heart.

"Who—are you?" he asked.

She leaned in close as she could to his face. "I'm the one who just fucking killed you." She pulled the demon dagger from his chest and stepped back to let the man collapse into the bane plague's tar. The muck rose up and devoured the Pilgrim in a blighted curse, swallowing up his screams, feasting on his death.

Black and red clouds swarmed at Lyra's feet. They spread out across the land, plucking the curses from all that remained, including what little energy was left of the demon. And then the smoke returned, filling Lyra with the weight of darkness. Armed her with the ability to carry it. Her body flooded with power at knowing its true name: The Girl Who Wasn't Fear.

She was no longer afraid. But they, Pilgrim and demon alike, would all fear her.

THE DEALINGS OF THORNS AND CROWS

ALEXIS L. CARROLL

A glass bottle shattered against the wall, its glittering shards showering down upon Milly. The golden liquid from inside stained the pure white fabric of her bonnet. She put her hands up to cover her ears as another bottle flew past her, but the sounds of the scuffle couldn't be blocked out so easily. Turning onto her hands and knees, she crawled toward the backside of the tavern's bar for safety.

How did I get in this mess?

A searing pain in her hand caused her to cry out, then quickly clap both hands over her mouth, lest she be heard. Once the urge to sob was gone she removed her hands and looked upon the one in pain. Biting down on her bottom lip, Milly wiggled loose the assailant, her palm pooling with ruby red blood. The glass had reopened an old wound and how she actually got into this mess came flooding back to her ....

"WHERE ON EARTH did you find this hellbane?" The high pitched whine of Beatrice commanded Milly's attention and she set aside the bouquet she was working on. The market wasn't noisy but Beatrice was extra loud anyhow. Such was her way.

Glancing around to see if anyone else had heard, Milly cleared her throat and leaned over the table to keep the plant's whereabouts a secret. "I found it in a glen in the middle of the woods, just beyond the old pond."

"She found it, she claims." Beatrice sneered over her shoulder at the two women who stood behind her. Sarah, an awkwardly tall, and curvaceous woman. And Tabitha, a short woman with a hooked nose. The three wore matching, fashionable chaperons and white aprons with embroidery of thorny vines along the bottom. One of Beatrice's many talents; cross-stitch. Their baskets were full with market treats already, making bullying Milly their final stop of the day. They disguised their laughter by coughing into handkerchiefs, but Milly knew all too well how many jokes they made at her expense. Since she had moved to the small, settler town with her father and nothing else, Milly had been picked on and made fun of by those three almost daily. And yet, it did not stop her from longing to be included in their circle.

Feeling particularly defiant to being the center of their jest, Milly stuck her chin out and gave a curt nod. "Indeed. And I found some monkshood." She hoped confidence would come out in her voice, but it was still the meek, soft-spoken tone people often mistook for a child's. The three women stared down their noses at her, unimpressed. She slunk her hand into her pocket, gripping a hidden metal trinket to calm her nerves. "I was . . . thinking of making . . . making a salve . . . well, a flying salve out of them."

The three let out terrible, unbridled laughter. No longer attempting to hide it. Beatrice nudged Sarah. Tabitha wiped at her eye, she was laughing so hard. At last Beatrice took a deep breath and calmed down. "A flying salve?! What is this? The Dark Ages?"

"Aye," Sarah chortled. "E'eryone knows ye cannit just make a flying salve spell."

Milly shrunk into herself, trying to escape their ridicule, and started putting her wildflowers and herbs away.

She was saved when the town's handsome new preacher walked up. Sunrays made his fair hair sparkle like spun gold and his cheeks were bronzed from the uphill walk to town. But the handsomest feature of all was the friendliest smile he always wore.

The women quietly swooned, turning their attention upon him. "Preacher Redmond," Beatrice cooed as she pushed past her friends to be front and center.

"Now, what have I said? Call me Tomas." Preacher Redmond flashed perfect, white teeth and sighs escaped the women. He looked at Milly, his smile broadening. "Closing up early this evening, Milly?"

Although she was enamored with the preacher like any other eligible person in the settlement, Milly flinched under his gaze. She liked to admire him from afar, in peace, but now she would have to deal with Beatrice and her cronies harassing her over yet another thing. She gave him a simple nod.

"Is that one last bouquet? Might I have it for my dining table tonight?" he inquired, leaning over the table to look at her wares. "Oh, unless one of you were purchasing it?"

Beatrice's smile was like that of a snake's and she dipped her head to the preacher, while elbowing her friends. "Oh, no. By all means, Tomas. That is all yours. Girls, say good-bye to our dear friend, *Mildred*."

"Good-bye, *Mildred*," the two crooned in unison.

The three left the market area, whispering in earnest just as soon as they were out of earshot. Milly shuddered to think about what they would do to her next time they got her alone.

"May I escort you some of the way home? I have to call upon the Edmontons to bless the new mother and infant, which I believe is on the way to your homestead."

Milly wasn't sure what she did to deserve the preacher's kindness, but she nodded. They walked in silence away from the marketplace, however it was not an uncomfortable silence. Just the presence of someone as calm as the preacher walking beside her filled Milly with a sense of belonging.

"You said the Edmontons had their baby?" Milly ventured to ask after a while.

"Yes, I am told a beautiful baby boy to carry on the family name," Preacher Redmond smiled, interlacing his fingers and resting his hands against his chest. "Do you have any interest? In children?"

Milly blanched. Children. Offspring. Someone to pass her knowledge unto. What little she even knew. Preacher Redmond was a young and bright eyed man of God, so his question seemed innocent enough. His sermons had nothing to do with the evils of devil worship, avoiding whispers from demons, and never had he even uttered a word about witches. And yet, she had to be wary.

Milly was a young witch, you see. Tragically, the gene had skipped two generations of women before her and all that was left of her heritage was in an old, faded grimoire she could hardly read. There was a small, local coven, but like most of the village, they shunned her for being of no important name. Beatrice may have also had something to do with it.

Preacher Redmond chuckled. "I suppose that's too private of a topic. Any young man would be lucky. I, myself, am considering a family soon enough."

"Is that so?" Milly responded politely, glad of the focus being taken off of her.

"Yes, although I think I may relocate to a town in a more desirable area. This town feels . . . a bit too small, too . . . gossipy."

You have no idea.

"You might consider a move yourself." He looked at her intently. "Here is where our paths part ways, I fear. Take care of yourself, Milly. Be sure to get home quick. It is a full moon tonight, I hear there are wolves in the woods. Oh, and do tell your father hello. We miss him on Sundays. Just a shame what befell him."

She dipped her head and gripped her baskets a bit tighter, but not out of fear. It *was* a full moon and that meant it was the most powerful night to perform magic. Wolves were no concern of hers.

That night she would touch the stars.

LEAVING her immobile father comfortable in a blanket beside the fire, his eyes closing, Milly packed her supplies into a basket and stepped out onto the porch. Dropping to her knees, she carefully lifted a floorboard and pulled out her great grandmother's grimoire. All she had left of the past. It was wrapped in layers of muslin, but they couldn't keep the scent of decay away. She gingerly put it into the basket.

The moon was near high enough to light her way through the woods as she scurried towards her destination. Pine needles and leaves crunched under foot, an occasional twig along with them, but other than that the forest was silent. Her heart sounded loud, beating hard against her chest from the exertion and excitement. She ignored the mean voices in the back of her head that sounded like Beatrice and her cronies, the ones saying she was nothing. That night she would be something.

The clearing was private, beautiful, serene, and she set about claiming the land for her spells. Walking barefoot an invisible barrier of four points, then connecting them in a circle. Slices of dried orange she laid North and South, then set her monkshood East and the hellbane West. In the center, a glass jar filled with oil. The grimoire felt perfect in her hands, like it belonged there. She flipped to the spell and started reciting the words. They fell from her lips, garbled and butchered no doubt. A long dead language. Nothing happened. Was something supposed to visibly happen? She scanned the page again, but because she could not fully understand the old tongue, she wasn't sure. A sigh of defeat escaped her as she watched the jar.

A crow flew down in a lazy circle towards the orange slice across from Milly. It started to peck at the fruit's flesh. "Hey," Milly called, but the crow ignored her. "HEY. That is MY offering." She crawled over and swatted at the crow with her grimoire, thinking it would fly off.

Thwack!

Stunned, Milly lifted the heavy book. Black feathers fell from its surface. On the ground lay a very smashed corvid. Its black leg twitched a few times then went still. "Oh, no.

Oh, no, no, no," she mumbled, horrified. "I'm sorry, little birdie."

"Sorry?" A deep voice vibrated throughout the clearing, shaking Milly through to the very bones. "Not very wicked of a witch, to be sorry."

Milly was speechless.

"Have you nothing else to say?" The dead crow's body twitched. "Would you let a sacrifice really go to waste?"

"Sacrifice?" Milly choked out, her eyes never leaving the crow that twisted in an unnatural way. It stood and cracked, turning its head back the right way. "Who are you? What do you mean?"

"All magic comes with a sacrifice, young one." Its beady black eyes stared her down. "Have you learned nothing?"

Milly shook her head, glancing at her grimoire in her lap. "I . . . I cannot read it. I have no teacher, no one to help me. I've just been . . . guessing."

The crow cocked its head this way and that, surveying the land. It clicked a few times, then hopped onto her shoulder. It leaned in close as it said, "You have natural talent, I can see, but you do need some guidance. Would you accept it?"

Milly chewed on her lip, rubbing her hands along the cover of her family's heirloom. "I don't even know who you are," she whispered, but she desperately wanted to do real magic. "What would you ask in return?"

"Clever girl," clucked the crow. "Give me something and I will show you how to do what you seek. What have you to offer?"

"I ha—have nothing," she stammered, but then remembered something. She reached into her skirt pocket and withdrew the calming trinket. Presenting the metal toy horse to the crow, Milly held her breath. Could she really part with it?

The crow pecked at the toy, its beak creating a clinking sound with each peck, like it was testing the metal. "This will do." It flapped its wings, snatched the toy in its claw, and flew up to circle around her. "The deal is done!" it cawed and disappeared into the night.

Milly waited in silence, waited for something to happen, for something to feel different. Nothing happened. She fretted she had given a mysterious talking crow her only childhood memorabilia. "I'm so *stupid*," she cried out as she stood up. The grimoire fell to the ground with a thud, flipped fervently through pages upon pages until it stopped. Milly bent down. At first there was no difference until the strange language became blurry. Or maybe her eyes had. She blinked several times, it did not clear, then rubbed at them. At last the words appeared and they were changed. She understood them. She understood and she knew what to do.

Excited barely touched how Milly felt as she tossed herself back onto the ground, hands on either side of the book, and she read the spell presented to her. The jar in the center of her sigil bubbled, steam rising out of it. The page flipped on its own and she continued reading, chanting the words in a clear voice. A wild wind whipped around the clearing and her offerings floated in the air. She recited another line. They spun round and round her. She finished the casting and they poofed into purple clouds. The area fell still. Her jar sat in front of her, filled with an intoxicating smell. Could it be? Her flying salve? She pulled the lid off and scraped her fingers along the thick concoction, then smoothed some along her hands. No sooner had she thought the word 'fly' when her hands lifted high into the air, pulling her off the ground. Her arms felt like they'd rip out of their sockets. "Ow! Down, down, down!" she cried out, the pain unbearable. Her feet hit the cold ground and she yanked her arms in, breathing hard.

Despite the pain, Milly rushed to remove her clothing with every intention of covering her whole body in the magical salve.

)❱●⊕●❰(

BY THE TIME Milly landed soundlessly on her porch, the girl's lips were blue and her naked body shook with chill. She had done it. She had flown home using old magic, magic that she hadn't known she could do but had always hoped for. Bubbles of joy burst inside of her, but the chattering of her teeth demanded she get inside. The door creaked as she entered and the wooden chair groaned when she set her basket down. Her father was snoring beside the dying fire, undisturbed and never the wiser. Even though it hurt her frozen fingers, Milly put her clothes back on and tossed two logs into the fireplace before she sat down with the grimoire nestled in her lap.

A world of new, powerful things would open up for her now that she could read the book. No longer would the local coven ignore her pleas to join. Beatrice and her cronies would *have to* respect her. And maybe, just maybe she could find happiness.

THE NEXT MARKET day Milly was abuzz with excitement. For the first time since moving to the New World's shores, she could not wait to see Beatrice, Sarah, and Tabitha. Her stall looked more amazing than it should have in the mid-Fall, thanks to a little glamor magic she had learned. She spent every free minute she had, between running the household and preparing for the once a week market day, studying the book's secrets. Unlocking all sorts of useful spells. Shrill laughter caught her attention and Milly stood straight, searching out the trio. She didn't have to wait long. They beelined right for her stall once they came into view.

"Well, well, well," Beatrice said, approaching the stall. The sneer on her face faltered and she scrutinized Milly more thoroughly.

Milly cleared her throat, nervous under the intense inspection. "See anything you like, Beatrice?"

Sarah stayed back, flabbergasted.

Tabitha walked from side to side, touching everything. Milly pulled a fragile stockpile of plants out of the way just in time.

"Look, girls," Beatrice hissed, regaining her composure. "The little mouse found her some magic after all."

Milly put on a brave smile and nodded once.

Tabitha leaned forward. "This is . . . is nearly seamless! It's even better than yours, B." She looked back at her leader who was quick to silence her with a sharp glare.

That made Milly smirk to herself. Of course old magic would be more impressive to people who had never seen it. "I even made my flying salve," Milly boasted. "The one you said couldn't be done. It was something wonderful to fly in a moonlit sky. The stars twinkled like diamonds."

"Wow," Tabitha breathed.

Sarah and Beatrice scowled at the same time and Sarah

shoved Tabitha behind them. "I don' believe it until I sees it."

"Aye," Beatrice agreed.

"I don't have any left." Milly reached into her pocket, but her calming trinket was gone. Traded to the crow. She missed it, but the ability she gained was better. An idea based off of the deal struck her. "I could teach you, all of you, if you like. If I were allowed to join the coven."

"The coven." Beatrice and Sarah spoke with one voice. They would be the hardest to convince. "You know the rules," Beatrice hissed. "We need to see that you're worthy, loyal, and strong."

"I am all of those things," Milly insisted. "Please. Give me a task. Any task. I'll do it!" She hadn't meant to sound so desperate.

The three huddled together, their hurried whispers intangible. At last they broke the circle and looked at Milly with matching smirks. Beatrice leaned forward. "Your first task is to produce water from stone."

Milly blinked, confused. "Water . . . from stone? But what does that even mean?"

Sarah grinned. "Ey, that's the thing," she said, full of confidence. "Ye have ta choose the best way ta show ye task with that there impressive magic."

Chewing on her lip, trying to think of what she could do, she looked at each woman before her. "And you all did these tasks, too?"

Tabitha nodded her head. "It's the rite of passage into the coven."

"Do you accept the challenge?" Beatrice asked.

There was no other choice. It did seem only fair to show she had power and knowledge to offer the coven. A coven was only as strong as its weakest member. And she knew that would be her. She gave a slow nod.

"Great!" Beatrice clapped her hands together. "You have forty-eight hours to present us with your task completion."

"Oh." Milly gulped, but Tabitha reached over and patted her hand before she could say more.

"You'll do fine." Tabitha pulled her hand back and the three turned to leave.

"This should be hilarious." Milly overhead Beatrice mutter under her breath.

) ❭ ● ◍ ● ❬ (

AT HOME, Milly mulled over ways she could make water from stone while she bathed and fed her father. She hadn't read enough in the thick grimoire for an idea to jump out at her and even though he was practically gone to the world, she didn't feel right looking at its secrets in her father's presence. Once he was settled with a quilt in front of the fire, his eyes heavy with sleep, she sat at the tiny table and flipped through the pages. She wished she knew what she was looking for. Tired, she rested her face in her hands.

Tap. Tap. Tap.

Milly glanced over at her father but he was sound asleep, only the crackle of the fire came from that direction.

Tap. Tap. Tap.

Slowly Milly stood, her sight set on the small window. A black crow's face appeared against the pane, flapping its wings, and startling her. Relief filled her as she rushed over and threw the window open. "Is it you? The creature that helped me before?"

"Caw, caw." The crow pecked at the window's edge,

splintering a piece of wood off. It twisted its head, looking at her.

"Please, I need your help," she whispered. "I need to find a spell to turn stone into water. Won't you help me?"

It remained quiet and still. Its beady black eyes bore into her. She knew what it needed. An offering.

"I . . . I have nothing left to give." She turned out her skirt pockets to show them empty. Turning a circle, she looked around the shabby cabin. Nothing of value. Not so much as shiny cutlery.

The crow pecked down on her hand, causing her to jump, then spoke. "Give me your flower stall and I will tell you how to do what you seek."

"My . . . flower stall?" It was such an absurd request, considering not only was a crow asking, but that her stall generated hardly enough to support herself and her father. What would she do without the stall? It was all she had. A once a week escape from the life of servitude she felt caring for her father. Biting on her lip, she turned away from the crow, her gaze landing on the grimoire. This was her destiny, she was sure of it. If she got in with the coven, they would provide for her the life she always wanted, always dreamed of. They would teach her the magic to sustain a better life. With a deep sigh, she gave a quick nod. "So be it, the stall is yours."

The crow gave a loud caw and once again the grimoire came to life, flipping through pages. The corvid flapped its wings. "The old quarry," it said between wing beats. "Go there, dig a deep hole, and use this spell."

Milly closed her eyes tight, the noise surrounding her too much for her ears. Then it stopped. The grimoire fell motionless, opened far into the pages. She walked over, confusion painted on her face. "A levitation spell?"

NO ONE VISITED the old quarry. It had been deemed barren and abandoned, a final resting place for boulders removed from properties. With her basket of supplies and a shovel, Milly left before sunrise to avoid being seen. *This is crazy.* She walked towards the center of the quarry. *What am I doing here? How is this going to work? Where do I even start?* As if answering her, clouds moved and a last sliver of the moonlight lit a spot. "Thank the Goddess," Milly whispered, bowing her head. She set her basket on a flat boulder, lit her lantern, and opened her grimoire to the marked spell. Taking a deep breath and reminding herself that this was the only way, she struck the shovel into the ground. It was met with resistance. She lifted the shovel again and put more effort into her strike. The earth was sliced into and Milly set forth digging a deep hole as the crow had instructed.

Dripping in sweat, Milly emerged from the hole. She was exhausted, but this was only one step completed. After scanning the words again, she turned towards the hole in the earth, lifted her hands palms out and recited. Nothing happened when she got to the end of the incantation. There was no tingle of magical power either. She pouted as she knelt beside the book and flipped the page. Maybe she forgot something. There it was. Mark items with the caster's blood.

Haven't I sacrificed enough? she thought.

Taking her gardening shears out, she slashed her hand and went around marking boulders in the area with her scarlet signature. A trail of her blood caught her eye and she hastily kicked the dirt into her hole. No signs of witchcraft left behind. The task done, Milly stood again in front of her hole, palms raised, and recited. A burning sensation that started at the gash traveled up her arm, into the other, and out her fingertips. The boulders around her quivered. Her eyes widened then she shut them tight to concentrate. As the words flowed from her mouth, and the boulders shook, more sweat broke out on her forehead. Loud crackling drew her eyes open and she watched the boulders at last lift into the air. She contained her excitement, forced herself to keep focus else they'd fall, and moved one hand. The motion guided one of the boulders in the same direction and Milly set about stacking the rocks around her hole, laying them to fit together like a puzzle.

When Milly moved closer to get a better view of the well wall she was building, the earth quaked beneath her. Confused, she looked into the hole and saw bigger boulders coming up, bumping into each other. *Oh no,* she thought and her lack of focus caused them to drop. *I must have enchanted them when I kicked the bloodied dirt down there.* Another sound reached her, a trickling at first, then a steady flow. Like a stream. Concentrating again, she levitated the boulders out and over her well. She made a quick flick of her wrist and sent them towards the old quarry's discarded pile, and with them the last of the spell. Again, she leaned in. The morning sun rays had found their way over the rock piles and into the well, creating a dazzling display on the water that continued to spill in.

"I did it," Milly muttered, aghast. "I made water from stone. I DID IT!" With a triumphant yell, she raised her fist into the air then danced around. She stopped, grinning from ear to ear, admiring her work. "And with time to spare. The sun is getting higher, I best run to Beatrice's before the day is half gone."

)◗●Ⓜ◀◀(

Beatrice, Sarah, and Tabitha trudged along behind an overzealous Milly. She tried her best to keep her emotions in check, but she nearly skipped the whole way back to the quarry. She couldn't help it. Her task was complete, it was beautiful, it was one step closer to coven acceptance.

They came across the church midway. Preacher Tomas Redmond was chopping firewood, his sleeves rolled up, exposing strong forearms. His sweat glistened in the afternoon sunlight, soaking his hair and collar. Beatrice bristled in front of Milly, eager to be noticed. A loud chop rang out and Tomas looked up. His gaze settled on Milly and a smile graced his handsome face.

"Why, Miss Milly, you have a healthy glow about you today," he said as he neared close to their path. He surveyed who she was with and tipped his head in acknowledgement. "Ladies. Out for a midday stroll?"

"Aye. We could not let such a day go to waste," Beatrice said in a sickeningly sweet tone. She stepped further in front of Milly, blocking the preacher's view. "I see you are hard at work."

Tomas wiped at his brow with a handkerchief. He looked at the two girls behind Milly, then back at Beatrice. "That I am." After putting the wet handkerchief into his pocket, he picked up his ax. "Back to it. Have a lovely day, ladies. Take care of one another."

He caught Milly's eye as they resumed walking and winked. She blushed and hurried along.

"Ooooh. That man," Tabitha said beside Milly once they were far from the church. "He is so delightfully good looking. And did you see those muscles?" A high pitched noise escaped her.

Sarah nodded in agreement, "Aye, whatta fine man he be. He could build a 'ouse with 'em arms, big enough for many wee ones."

"Shush, you two," Beatrice hissed as they neared the quarry. "Why are we here?"

"What even is this place?" Tabitha inquired.

"Innit the old 'arry? Me da worked here for'a time." Sarah looked unimpressed. A rock underfoot caused her to stumble and Milly couldn't help but smirk.

"I picked this location—" Milly fumbled to carefully choose her words. "—because what better way to show my capabilities than to bring you water out of the rocky terrain deemed barren to society."

When the well came into sight, the sun shined down at the perfect angle, reflecting off the water that had filled to the top of the hole. Milly kept her face devoid of surprise at its level and remained back as the other three circled around the well, inspecting. For a brief second, she had a dark fantasy of the wall crumbling into the water, taking her tormentors with it as they leaned over the side. It was gone as fast as it came, and she smiled when Beatrice looked at her.

"I have to hand it to you, *Mildred*, this is . . . fairly good." Beatrice shrugged and Sarah nodded. But it was Tabitha that dared to lean farther over the well, one foot in the air, and touch the water. She lifted her fingers to her mouth and tasted.

"This is divine!" she squealed. "Why, it tastes as if it had fallen from a mountain spring. How ever did you do it, Milly?"

Milly cleared her throat, unused to the praise. "Just . . .

wanted to complete the coven task while also creating something useful."

Beatrice smirked and moved to stand face to face with Milly. "One task done, one more to go."

Sarah and Tabitha followed behind them, making Milly feel like she was trapped as she followed Beatrice back towards town. The thought of what they would require her to do next hung over her head like an unknown phantom.

They ended at Milly's homestead, Beatrice turning sharp on her heel to face Milly again. "I don't know what kind of magic you're using that has made you all of a sudden good," Beatrice growled, poking Milly in the chest. "But I cannot deny it has been impressive. That's why, for your next task . . ."

Milly's heart hammered. Beatrice's nostrils flared, something Milly noticed she did when she was mad at the other girls. She had gotten under the brute's skin. It took all her strength to not smile.

"Your next task is . . ." Beatrice repeated and her gaze darted at the woods. "To kill two giants."

"Giants?" Tabitha quipped, but Sarah nudged her silent.

Milly gulped. "D-d-do giants exist?"

Beatrice tutted then nodded her head to signal the other women to follow her. "For your sake, *Mildred*, you better hope so. You have forty-eight hours."

A miserable sigh escaped Milly as the women disappeared down the path to town. Each step to her cabin felt heavier than the last and thoughts of where or even how to find one giant, let alone two, sped through her mind. The tasks were getting harder and harder. Was it because that was the coven way? Or was this another form of torture Beatrice had worked up?

The cabin enveloped her in warmth and the sight of her

father cozy by the fire lifted her spirits. Comfort in the expected. Safety in the familiar. Her wooden chair creaked when she plopped down into it and rested her head in the crook of her arm. "What have I gotten myself into? Father, what would you say?" She turned her head and stared at the back of his head, wishing, hoping for a miracle. "'You've come this far, not for naught, haven't you?'" Milly answered in a mock-deep voice, the closest she'd get to him replying. "'And you aren't alone, are ye? You've got me.'"

The reality that she had near no one stung. She turned away from her father to stare into the woods. A shadow passed by. Perking up, Milly straightened. "Maybe I'm not so alone," she muttered, waiting for the crow to appear at the window. When nothing happened, she rushed out to the porch and looked skyward. No sign of the thing. "Please, crow! I *need* your assistance once more! I have the most impossible task and you've been so helpful with the others."

Silence.

Disheartened, she returned inside to start their supper.

) ❭❭❶❺❶❬❬ (

With the timeline hanging over her head, Milly went to market to purchase food for the house, and if she was lucky, hear any rumors she could about possible giants. It was quiet as farmers were still setting up in the early hours. She looked over some herbs while the stall owner chatted with his neighbor.

"Did you hear all that ruckus last night?"

"Goodness, yes. What was it about?" The other stall owner leaned over, wiping her hands on her apron.

Milly moved a little closer to listen.

"Those new folk, the brothers, have been at the tavern every night," the man said. "Apparently once they hit the drink too hard, the littlest of things set em off. Noisy fights the owner can't stop."

"Terrible, just terrible that people like that would move to town," the woman sighed.

Milly also sighed and flagged the stall owner to pay. As she dropped the coin into his calloused hand, time seemed to slow down and the beat of wings surrounded her. A shadow flew overhead. Could it be? Time sped back up along with her heart. "Thank you!" She tipped her head then darted towards where the shadow disappeared. Around the corner she saw it. The crow. *Her* crow. It sat on a barrel, staring right at her, waiting for her. "You heard my plea," she said, breathless. The crow flapped its wings and took off, soaring down the lane, and she followed.

"Please! Wait up!" she called, barely keeping her footing and the black corvid in her sights. It turned and she followed. "Oof!" Milly was sent flying backwards when she crashed into someone. Her basket of things went up in the air, its contents raining all around her.

"Oh, no! I am sorry, Milly. Let me help you."

Preacher Tomas Redmond's soft hand latched onto hers and pulled her up, worry plain on his face. "Are you alright? I was hoping to see you, but not literally bump into you."

Her cheeks burning from a blush, Milly was rendered speechless being so close to him. She slid her hand from his and stepped back, looking away. "Oh, it's fine. I was not looking where I was going," she muttered. When she saw her things on the ground, she hurried to pick them up. Her grimoire had been in the basket but was now nowhere in sight. A panic rose up in her. "Oh, no. No, no, no."

"Looking for this?" Tomas held the book out for her.

"Yes," she said, careful to not sound too eager. He had no idea what he held in his hand. "It . . . was my great grandmother's herbology book. The notes are handwritten, you see. A drop of water would erase its knowledge forever." She was quick to place it back into the bottom of her basket, covering it up with its muslin cloth.

"Milly, I wanted to talk to you about yesterday."

"Oh?" Milly's heart stopped. Had he seen the well?

"Yes, I don't mean to pry, but this new development of friendship with Beatrice . . . it has me a little concerned. Is everything alright?"

A sigh of relief escaped her and she nodded her head. "Yes, it is all well and fine. Those three women are helping me out."

"With?" he inquired, no sign of leaving her be.

She was not aware he knew that they had not gotten along. Beatrice was sneaky with her bullying, careful to never show her true nature around others. Milly needed a lie, a good lie that this observant preacher would believe. "Cross-stitch." It was the only believable thing that came to her. "Yes, cross-stitch. Since I've sold my stall, I needed something new to bring an income for my father and I. And Beatrice's patterns are notoriously beautiful."

His features went from curious to worried again. "You sold your stall? Why? To whom?"

The sound of wings flapping, and his questions, made her anxiety spike. Milly had to get back to following the crow. Who knew if it would wait for her to catch up. And Tomas's questions were getting too hard to answer, too many lies she would have to keep up with. Her hands started to shake. Black tail feathers caught her eye. "I . . . I . .

. I am sorry, but I really must be going," she stammered then rushed past him.

By the time she caught up to the crow again, Milly was on the side of town unaccompanied women should never be. She looked around, worried, until she spotted the crow sitting atop a sign. The tavern. She went into the alley beside it. "Why have you led me here, crow? Do you know the kind of trouble I could be in?"

The crow hopped down in front of her, twisting its head in different ways to peer at her, then tapped at the glass window.

"Stop that," Milly hissed. "I don't want to be seen." But she leaned closer to look through. The window was too dirty to see. She pulled out her handkerchief and scrubbed a circular peeping hole. Trying not to press her face against the glass, Milly gazed around the tavern's main area. She had never seen inside before. "What am I looking for, bird?" she whispered. Before the bird even had time to answer, if it would, a loud bang and a door to the side of the tavern's drinking room opened. The tallest man Milly had ever seen in her life ducked down to step out, followed by another tall man, almost identical in looks. Two disheveled women leaned against the door frame, waving them off, though they both looked glad to be rid of them.

"Those must be the new brothers I heard about," Milly said, watching them. "Is that what you want me to see? Disgusting men leaving the scene of defilement?"

"Oh, don't be such a Puritan," the crow cackled. "Look at them. Are they not giants amongst men?"

The realization of what that meant hit Milly. She took a step back. Her hand fluttered to her throat. "You . . . you want me to *kill them*? Humans?"

The crow scoffed.

"I cannot, no. I simply cannot."

"Tell that to the coven then." The crow pecked her hand. "Tell them you are too *weak*. That you traded your beloved trinket, traded your livelihood, only to give up on the final task."

The air around her was too thin, panic started to take over. But the crow was right. She did not sacrifice all of that just to surrender. Leaning out to catch sight of the brothers leaving, Milly questioned when her morals had become so easily swayed. *They are troublemakers,* she reasoned with herself. With a heavy sigh, she closed her eyes and said, "Tell me what I must do."

"Meet back here after the sun sets!" The crow called as it set off into the sky. It dropped a smooth stone at her feet.

"I can do this," she muttered, trying to convince herself as she picked the unusual gift. Milly had never murdered anyone, let alone two people.

) ◗ ● ⓜ ◖ ◖ (

DREAD CREPT inside every ounce of Milly's being, making her journey back to the tavern in the cover of evening, difficult. Painfully aware that each step she took was a death sentence for innocent men. Her only comfort was that it would be the final task. She would never have to prove herself in such a way again. Her father and her could live happily together and she would have a coven-family. Other witches to practice her craft with. She would belong.

Music floated out of the tavern, upbeat and reverberant, accompanied by laughter. The night was jovial, nowhere near how she felt. Again she went to the alley beside the establishment. "Crow," she whispered. "Crow, I am here.

What will you have me do? What spell will help me achieve this task? Oh, please, let it be a quick, painless death for those two souls." She was met with silence, no sign of the corvid.

Hours went by that Milly spent flipping through her grimoire, the smooth rock gripped in her free hand. She was not even sure what she could offer the crow. The very clothes off her back, perhaps. When more time had passed, she decided to take matters into her own hands. Taking a deep, shaky breath, Milly worked up some courage and unbuttoned her top to expose just enough bosom. *What am I doing!* She panicked, but hiked up her skirt anyway. She had never been so immodest in public. She rolled her sleeves as she approached the entrance. A cheer went up in the tavern. Milly used it as a distraction to sneak inside.

Carefully she slinked over to the bar, reaching a jittery hand over to grab a bottle. Turning, she sought out the means to end her task. The brothers sat at separate tables, deep into games of dice. She wondered if they were working the room, robbing the townsmen of their hard earned coins. She hoped so; anything to justify killing them. She went to the one closest to her, putting on a brave face. "Gent, you look like you could use another drink," she said, too softly and it went ignored. She cleared her throat loudly and leaned heavily against the tall man, making her bosom front and center. "I said, how abouts another drink, handsome?"

"Ooooh, don't mind—" his eyes roamed her body. "—if I do, little lady. My, you are a fresh one tonight, aren't you?"

A giggle left Milly's lips, though she cringed inwardly. She would have to sage her whole naked being under the next new moon. She poured him a drink and lifted away when it was his turn. Quick as could be, she went to the other brother and repeated the process. As she turned to leave him, he grabbed her around the waist and Milly squeaked. She pushed at him, but laughed. "Oh, good sir, I'm afraid I'm spoken for."

"Nonsense!" He laughed and pulled her close. "I'll pay double! You smell like honeysuckle on a spring day! No way I'll let anyone else taste that before me."

As repulsed as she was, she tried to appear flattered. "Ah, but it is a good amount this one offers. 'Tis that man, over there. Your brother."

Please take the bait.

He glanced over his shoulder at his brother then made a face. "Bah, that sunnuffa hound? I'll just wrestle him for you. Be a dear, go en pour him anotha drink and tell him I get firsts."

It was working, her plan to pit the two against each other in a jealous rage. She went right away to the other table, plopping herself boldly on the brother's lap. She batted her eyes.

"Lady, you sure know how to grab attention, dontcha? You're in luck." He spat a little as he talked. "I won big tonight. And that means, so do you."

"Oh dear, but then what would I tell your brother? He's already paid me, in full."

"Trust me, you don't want to touch that blighted fool. Now, go tell him he can have Virginia tonight after all. You are all mine until the sun comes up." He pushed her off and towards his brother.

Milly wondered just how much more back and forth, vulgar talk she'd have to endure before they got into an actual fist fight over her. She had a new respect for the ladies of the night that worked there. They put up with some awful mistreatment and Milly resolved herself to befriend each and every one, offering them any assistance her magic could conjure up, once she was in the coven. They deserved better. As for herself, she'd need saging *and* a swim in the crystal clear lake to be rid of the grime their hands left.

The bottle of liquor in her hand was near empty by the time one brother had had enough and stood with an attention-grabbing screech of his chair. He lumbered past Milly, towards his brother, and she watched with bated breath as the man yanked his brother's chair out and shook him. He yelled drunken gibberish, the words unintelligible to the rest, but his brother's face turned red and he stood.

"How dare you!" he slurred and shoved his brother off. He went to get Milly, but was jerked back by the collar. He was ready, however, and took a swing at his brother the moment they were once again face to face. The hit missed, landing on the wooden table, disturbing the other gamblers. They all stood up, hollering and whooping, clearly enticed by the fight.

Milly jumped out of the way as a chair slid across the floor. Her plan to pit them against each other worked better than she had imagined. Soon the fight between the two had the whole tavern enthralled and they surrounded the brothers, though Milly could see them towering over the rest, taking swings and missing. When the misses started to find new targets, the other patrons got rowdier and joined in. Angry yells and balled up fists took over. Tables were being crashed into, chairs destroyed. Milly backed up toward the bar, terrified of being caught in the center of the fighting. Someone stole the bottle from Milly's hand, which she was glad to be rid of, and she ducked to the floor just as they made to grab for her. Behind the bar seemed the safest place for her, at least until she could escape out the side door. But the brothers. She glanced behind her and spied the two struggling.

A glass bottle shattered against the wall, its glittering shards showering down on top of her pure white bonnet. The golden liquid inside burned her eyes and nostrils. She put her hands up to cover her ears as another bottle flew past her, but the sounds of the scuffle couldn't be blocked out so easily. She crawled toward the backside of the tavern's bar.

How did I get in this mess? she wondered in dismay.

A searing pain in her hand caused her to cry out, then quickly clap both hands over her mouth, lest she be noticed. Once the urge to sob was gone she removed her hands and looked at the one in pain. She bit down on her bottom lip and wiggled loose a piece of glass. Ruby red blood pooled in her palm. The glass reopened an old wound and how she got to this scene came flooded back to her.

More blood sacrifices, she thought and looked around. *Where is that blasted—*

Above her, appearing out of nowhere, the crow stood. Its black feather's soaked up the candlelight. It quirked its head and peered at her from one eye, and the scene with the other.

"What a mess you have made," it said.

"A mess *I* made?" Milly hissed. "You were supposed to meet me. I need your help, quick! We must stop this madness. I never meant for more people to get involved."

The crow dipped its head and lapped at some spilled ale. "What will you give me in return?"

The question she had been dreading. "Crow, all I have left is the clothes on my back. Will that do?"

"Nay," the crow cawed. It leaned down, looking her in the eye. "Give me your father."

"My—my father?" She was mortified. "No! What use have you for my father? He was stricken down in his prime by a stroke. Why, he cannot even speak anymore. No, absolutely not."

The crow said nothing, merely stared at her. Another crash from furniture being broken. A man was tossed over the bar, hitting the back wall with a thud. He jumped back, grabbed a bottle and broke its body against the bar. That's when he noticed Milly cowering.

She leaned back farther away from him. Her mind and heart raced. Why would the crow want her father? Maybe she didn't need the crow's help. She had hoped this plan would end in them killing each other. The man leered at her, his intent written all over his face. Fear filled her. The crow cawed beside her, but the man paid no notice.

"Fine!" Milly shouted as she scrunched back against the wall. "Just help me!"

"The rock I gave you," the crow said. "Hurry and repeat these words: *luas à cloch dul.* And throw it."

Taking a quick deep breath, Milly pulled the rock from her skirt pocket. "*Luas à cloch dul.*" Closing her eyes tight, she threw the rock as hard as she could. A wet, bone crushing sound followed. A gruesome sight was before her when she opened her eyes. Blood seeped out of a thick hole in the center of the man's skull. Milly gasped, scrambling to pull herself away from the blood. A thud sounded on the other side of the bar, then another, and another. The clatter of the fighting lessening. She reached a shaky hand up where the crow used to be and peered over.

The smooth rock flew through the air as well as anything in the way, like an insect from human to human, leaving a trail of bodies in its wake. Patrons of the tavern fell dead none the wiser to their demise. It was too gruesome for Milly and she ducked down, covering her mouth to keep the screaming inside. This was not what she had planned, nor even thought could happen. She was barely willing to kill the brothers, now she had the blood of a tavern full of people on her hands.

After the room had been silent for a few minutes, Milly dared to peek over again. Unmoving cadavers, their blood seeping out, soaking every inch of the floor. She carefully moved around the body behind the bar, around the other bodies, looking for the intended targets. There they were, close to where she had left them. The brothers were frozen in time interlocked together, immortalized in her memory.

A distant cawing shook the shock away and Milly rushed out of the tavern, going to the alley for her things. The sun would soon come up and it was imperative that no one saw her there. There were only three people that needed to know she had been there. The massacre would be the talk of the town within hours upon discovery. She had to get home. Determined to see her father one last time. Or maybe even prevent the crow from taking him at all.

) ❱ ● Ⓜ ◀ ◀ (

"FATHER!" Milly crashed into the cabin, out of breath. She went to his chair by the fireplace and slid to the floor, finding naught but a scrap of his quilt. Clutching it close to her heart, tears streamed down Milly's dusty cheeks and an unbearable ache gripped her heart. She was too late. "Father, I'm sorry," she wailed. "I'm sorry! I didn't . . . I didn't mean for it to be this way! Please! Please, bring him back!" Slumping to the floor in a heap, Milly curled into a ball and wept and wept and wept until she fell into a deep slumber.

)◗●◍◖((

A TAPPING at the window awoke Milly in the late evening. A dark shadow preened itself outside. The memory of why she was on the floor and exhausted flooded back to her. *The crow. My father.* She scrambled to get out the door.

"You did well. Are you not pleased with yourself?" The crow cocked its head. "Are you not a powerful witch now, coven-bound?"

"Not like this," she croaked. "It was a mistake. I take it back. I want my father back."

Caw!

The crow flapped its wings in a flurry. "You ungrateful child!" it yelled, flying over her head. "I unlocked the greatest, oldest of magic for you and you *dare* call it a mistake? You cannot take back the lives you have undone. We traded, fair and square."

Milly's heart sunk deeper within and tears formed. "What do you want? Another trade?" There was nothing left to give the crow, but she had to try.

It landed on her shoulder, interested, and gave a gentle nibble on her ear. "What do you offer? What could you ever offer in exchange for all that I have taken?"

"I . . . I don't know. What do you want, crow? My house? My . . . my life?"

The crow clucked its tongue in thought. "Hmm . . . I've an idea, a game of sorts. If you can guess my name, you may have everything back and keep the magic knowledge. If you cannot, I keep everything, and your soul."

"My soul?" Milly gripped her chest, thinking. Souls were powerful things, even with her limited experience, she knew that possessing someone's soul could create the strongest, darkest magic.

"Yes, your soul," the crow replied as it climbed to her other shoulder. "Your . . . little . . . bitty . . . soul. But, if you can figure out my name, you get the better deal. You get your trinket back, your livelihood, your father."

"It's a deal," she whispered.

"Excellent." The crow leapt off her and into the air. As it flew off, it called back, "You have forty-eight hours to solve this, child."

) ◗ ● Ⓜ ◖ ◀ (

ON THE FIRST DAY, Milly sat on the porch edge, watching the crow hop around below her, as she guessed any and all names that came to her. "Oliver? William? John? George?"

The crow tsked and stopped to scratch at the ground.

"Bart. Frederick. Gideon. Charles. Marius. Hector. Edmund. Linus. Please, crow. Am I even close? Can you not give me a little hint?"

"A hint was not in our agreement," the crow replied, not even bothering to look at her. "I am tired of this for today. You have until tomorrow evening, Mildred. Or I will collect your soul next."

With that, it flew away and left Milly alone. Her tears fell heavy and hot, the despair within her all consuming. Its last words rang in her head over and over. The time limit in which to discover a crow's name was unfair and cruel. The cruelest joke someone could play. She chewed on her bottom lip, thinking. Something formed in her thoughts, a last grasp. *Mildred* the crow had called her. Calling her that, along with the cruelty of the situation, reminded her of someone. Someone who might help.

"LET ME IN! Let me in right this moment!"

Milly pounded on the door, tear-streaked and unkempt hair barely contained under the white bonnet. There was no time for bathing, no time for formality. Her father's life was on the line. And her soul.

"Mildred! What is the meaning of this!"

Milly tried to push the door open when Beatrice opened it a crack, but Beatrice leaned hard against it, a scowl upon her face. And something underlying, just behind her eyes. *Fear.*

"Oh, do let her in, B," Tabitha called from inside. "She's done the tasks. She's part of the coven now."

Beatrice grimaced but moved aside, allowing Milly to enter into the warm parlor. Tabitha and Sarah sat in wooden chairs close together, working on a cross-stitch pattern. Tabitha waved, but Milly did not return it. Instead, she turned on her heel and fell to her knees. Gripping the hem of Beatrice's apron, with the fine thin stitched row of thorns, Milly looked up and pleaded. "Please, I need your help. Do you know of the crow? Of the magic it offers? I know you do, you must, you must," she babbled. "Please. I need its name. It has my father and now it wants my soul. I . . . I . . . I . . ." The tears took over once again.

Beatrice made a disgusted face. "I don't know what you're talking about."

"Oh." As if struck, Milly fell back from Beatrice's lap and covered her face with her hands as she wept more.

"Oh, hogwash Beatrice." Tabitha stood from her chair, taking the project with her. "I cannot stand to lie any longer. Milly, girl. Clean yourself up." She handed the white cloth to Milly.

Turning it over in her hands, Milly realized what it was. An apron with the thorn pattern along the edge.

"You *are* one of us now," Tabitha said.

"Aye," Sarah added, standing. "Ye are. But ye still 've gotta prove ye'self for in—in—"

"Don't hurt yourself, Sarah," Beatrice spat then leaned down and gripped Milly by the shoulders. "This kind of information we cannot give freely."

"Please, I'll do anything."

Tabitha moved beside them and nodded. "We have a special task for you. The final task."

Drenched by the sudden rains, Milly stood outside of the church's door with her heart pounding and nerves shot. She lifted her hand to knock but the door opened before she worked up the courage. Preacher Tomas Redmond stared down at her, confused, and she was equally flustered by his lack of attire. His bronze chest looked so strong and inviting, like a single hug from him could warm her head to toe.

"Milly? What is it? Why are you here at this hour?"

"I have a favor to ask. A life or death situation," she whispered, wishing there was any other way.

His gaze softened and he ushered her inside the church.

"Is it your father? Come, we can pray for his health together."

"No!" Milly's word rang out in the tiny building. "What I meant is, yes, it does have to do with my father. But I need your help in a . . . a . . . a different way."

"How can I help you?" He rested his hand upon her arm.

"I need you to pretend to be . . . in love . . . with me." She could hardly breathe and shook all over. "And . . . and it has to be convincing or I'll never get what I need for my father."

"Oh." He glanced away.

Milly bit her lip, scared he'd never agree or that he'd ask more questions. But she couldn't do what they asked. She would never put a love spell on him. He was too kind, especially to her when no one else was. "I'm sorry. I promise I won't ask for anything from you ever again. Just this once."

He removed his hand from her arm and lifted her face up towards his. Their eyes locked. When his head moved closer to hers, her eyes fluttered close, and their lips met in a warm, unexpected kiss.

Tomas pulled away after a moment and said, "I do not need to pretend."

"Milly! Are you home, Milly?"

Still bubbling from the night before, Milly awoke from her slumber with a new sense of hope and belonging, near overpowering the anxiety she had been under. Leaving her father's chair, she fixed her bonnet and picked up the new apron from the table, tying it as she went to the door. The person outside pounded on the door. Opening it, Milly saw

Tabitha standing before her. Her face flushed, like she had run there. Behind her the sun was rising.

"What are you doing here? I thought I was going to meet Beatrice this morning," Milly asked, then grinned. "And tell her of my success!"

Tabitha appeared surprised. "Oh, wow. That is amazing. What spell did you use? Oh, nevermind. You have to hear what I have to say, and quick."

Not about to tell Tabitha there was no spell, only true love, Milly moved aside to allow Tabitha entrance and closed the door. "What is so important?"

"Beatrice was never going to give you the information," Tabitha breathed, plopping down onto a chair at the table.

"What? What do you mean? We had a deal. One more task." Panic rising, Milly's hands shook as she reached for the back of a chair to steady herself. "I've done all she's asked. Terrible things, even!"

Tabitha held up her hand. "I know. Powerful things. That's why she won't give you the information. You're too much competition for her. There's no doubt you would surpass her and the elders would make you a coven leader. Milly, I like you. That is why I am here to tell you what she will not. About the demon of the woods, the demon who has been using you."

Milly stood frozen.

Demon.

"He is a trickster demon." Tabitha lowered her voice. "Knowing his name will release the bond tied to you."

"Tell me," Milly whispered.

"You must never repeat it after using it to free yourself, never. For saying it again will summon him back. His name . . ." She glanced around the house, then leaned closer to

Milly, sliding a piece of paper over. Written in fine scrawl; *Martnign Sol.*

Milly locked the name into her memory.

A far off cawing unnerved both the women and they looked at the window. Nothing was there. Tabitha stood abruptly and headed towards the door. "I have to go now, before Beatrice wonders where I am." She paused half out the door. "Good luck, Milly. I am rooting for you."

"Thank you," was all Milly could say. Now that she had the key to free herself, waiting for the crow's return would take the little patience she had left.

It was not very long, luckily, until the crow appeared and tapped the glass, summoning her forth. Stepping onto the porch, Milly did her best to seem anxious and helpless, like she wasn't about to spoil the demon's plans.

"Well, child. Are you ready to try guessing again? This is your last chance to free yourself and your father."

"Please, crow! A hint? I have spent all the waking and resting hours thinking of names."

The crow walked along the wood, its talons clicking as it did. Milly took a deep breath and began to recite names. She planned on holding out until the crow tired. After all the torment the beast had done to her, she would drag out its game. It was hard not to watch the disguised demon closely, to analyze its moves. How had she missed it was a demon? It looked like an ordinary crow.

"Dillion. Tyrel. Kelly. Charles."

"No, no, no, and no. Gods, those are such boring names." The crow jumped onto her head and pecked. "Have you anything more unique, more fun!"

"I am trying, crow," Milly sighed. "Please—"

Peck. Peck. Peck.

"No hints! No hints! Just guess! I tire of you, child!"

'Good, and I tire of you,' Milly thought and prepared for what might come next. She stood, forcing the crow to flap off. It landed in front of her and walked around. "How about . . . Mmm-Martha?"

The crow stopped, turning his head towards her.

"No, that's not it. Maybe . . ." Milly tapped her chin, thinking. "Mmm-Marigold."

Flapping its wings hard, the crow got close to Milly's face but she backed away before it could peck. It let out a terrible caw. This was her only chance, otherwise the beast might try to destroy her before she could say more.

"Crow. I know your name and I know your game. Today, you shall not have my soul. And you *will* return my father." This time the confidence Milly always sought rang true. "Thy name be *Martnign Sol*, demon!"

The crow's head shot straight up, its black beak opened wide in a voiceless shriek, and its feathers started to fall away. Its body grew, grew, grew, then it shrunk, shrunk, and shrunk, and soon it was smaller than a chick. It gargled then let out a single, twisted caw before it blinked out of existence with a powerful boom that sent Milly flying back. Black feathers rained down upon her. The ordeal was done. She'd won.

) ▶ ● Ⓜ ◀ ◀ (

DAYS HAD PASSED PEACEFULLY by the time Milly was summoned to her first official coven meeting. As she walked the path to a new location she'd never been, she thought about how great her life had become since defeating the demon. Her father was returned to her, a little rougher for the wear, but alive nonetheless. And, to her surprise, Tomas had remained true about his feelings for her and visited often. She no longer felt alone.

When she arrived, Milly felt an invisible barrier send a tingling sensation throughout her body. *I have to learn that one,* she thought as she moved past it. Looking around, she noted the clearing where the coven met was devoid of plant life. *Sacrifice.* Cloaked people stood around talking, hardly noticing her, and she wished for a familiar face amongst the hidden crowd.

"Milly!" Tabitha waved, removing her hood as she stepped out from behind someone. "Over here."

Making her way amongst the mystery coven members, she hurried to Tabitha. The figures beside her lowered their hoods. Beatrice had a sour face and Sarah mirrored her, however with less vinegar.

"Sisters." Milly dipped her head in greeting.

"Tch." Sarah rolled her eyes.

"Mildred, we're glad to see you survived." It sounded like Beatrice had to force her words to sound civil.

"No thanks to you," Milly muttered.

"Eh, what didda ye say?!" Sarah stepped close to Milly but Tabitha pushed them apart.

"Coven members! Attention!" A deep voice broke the tension, clapping to demand all attention. "We're here today to welcome our newest, most promising member." They motioned to Milly, stepping aside to let her stand center as well.

Clearing her throat, she pushed forth her new confidence. "Thank you, brethren, but I have some unfortunate news. As kind—" She looked pointedly at Beatrice and Sarah. "—as your offer of fellowship and mentorship is, I am afraid I will be turning it down and handing this over." She untied the apron from her waist, folding it gingerly and walking to Beatrice. "I've a better offer. One I could not refuse."

"Are you sure about this?" the leader asked. "Once you say no to us, there is no turning back."

"I fought tooth and nail to get into this coven," Milly proclaimed, gripping the apron. "But I cannot turn down following the person I love. Preacher Redmond has asked for my hand in marriage and we're to move to a brand new settlement."

Beatrice rested her hand on the apron, but did not take it. Instead she looked over at the leader. "We've been meaning to expand our community, have we not? Would this not be a great opportunity to do such a thing? And, we cannot deny that Milly would be a strong coven leader."

She used my name.

Beatrice, someone who had been her enemy for so long. Never had she been complimented in such a way, never had she been offered so much responsibility and power. She looked around at the cloaked coven members, waiting for someone to protest, to say she was unworthy.

"That is a great idea," the leader agreed. "What do you say, Milly? Will you lead a division of our coven for the witches of this new settlement?"

A squeeze of her hand brought her gaze back to Beatrice who was smiling at her.

Milly grinned as well. "I would be honored."

) ❭ ● ◍ ◀ ❬ (

THEY WATCHED Milly disappear over the hill after the meeting had ended. "Do ye think she suspects?" Sarah asked.

Tabitha shook her head. "No, not at all. Where is she going anyway, Beatrice?"

"A settlement in Massachusetts," Beatrice replied, still grinning. "A place called Salem."

The leader stepped up behind the three women and placed its hands upon Beatrice and Tabitha's shoulders. "You three did well guiding her."

"Thank you, Lord Martnign Sol," the trio replied.

GREED

ALEXIS L. CARROLL

"Ugh. Somebody kill me," Hector groaned. "Where am I?"

His head spun as he sat up and a metallic residue coated his tongue. Something crusted in the corners of his mouth. All he could remember was dancing, booze, and the new clan he was initiated into celebrating. Hector had been charged with guarding the VIP section. The rest was fuzzy.

He groaned again and ran a hand over his face, pushing some sunglasses up into the tangled mess of his black hair. Elbow bumping into the steering wheel, Hector realized he was in a car, which was unusual since he didn't own one. And he wasn't blood-starved, like he often was first waking. Flipping down the visor mirror, he inspected himself. As suspected, evidence of a recent meal remained on his tan lips. He licked at the corner, barely reaching the dried blood. It was then he noticed his watch was missing.

"Dammit!" He slammed his fists against the steering wheel and turned to the passenger seat. Not at all surprised by the drained corpse of a woman. "Don't suppose you took my watch? Or have some wet wipes in here?"

Helping himself, he popped open the glove compartment and dug around, finding parking tickets, an old MP3 player, some half dried up hand sanitizer. No wipes, no watch. Next he inspected the small purse in the center of the console, hoping his blood donor had maybe stolen the watch. Instead he only found a wad of cash and a pocket knife. Cash went into his jean pockets and he flipped the blade out. "This was useful, huh?"

The corpse didn't respond.

He chuckled at his own dark humor and opened the car door. He stepped out into a rundown, wooden barn. "Where the hell am I?" Try as he might, he could barely recall the night before. Relieved of his guard duties around midnight, he had gone hunting for a bite in the shady New York City nightclub.

"Sleep tight, Hector," a fading voice echoed over and over in his mind, his eyes getting too heavy to keep open. There was a shocking slap to his face and someone shoved sunglasses onto him. 'Don't let the sun get ya.' A car door slammed and he succumbed completely to the blackness of sleep.

Who had spoken to him was a mystery, though he had a sneaking suspicion who it could be. A rumbling from below his feet dashed the memory fragments away and he fought to keep balance while the ground shook. "Ay! Earthquake?!" Hector had never experienced one before. They had done drills in grade school, but that was long ago. What was it he was supposed to do first? Hide under a desk?

Cracking and crumbling sounds filled the barn as the earth shook even harder. Hector turned to jump back into the car for safety. Before he could open the door, the ground split in two, creating a wide pit and the car fell with a sickening crunch. The horn blared, inflicting a searing headache, and he shielded his ears. The victim's final feeble cry from the grave.

The earth rumbled a third time, knocking Hector back into a pile of hay as a large, dark beast flew out from the pit. It flapped enormous bat-like wings as it darted around, trapped under the barn's roof. It seemed like the noise was messing with its sense of direction as it crashed into the ceiling again and again.

Hector had never seen a creature like it. It was a wondrous, terrifying thing to behold. Finally the beast stopped and let out a mighty shriek. "ENOUGH FOUL SPAWN!" It roared, swooping down upon the car. Digging its claws into the metal roof, the beast thrashed around, desperate to end the noise coming from the car.

Hector slinked out from the hay, scurrying in the cover of objects and their shadows to get a closer look. Black leathery wings were half-raised masts, with a sharp dew claw at the center. Tight muscles rippled under the oil slick rainbows of its black scales, showing little strain as it ripped through layers of metal. Its long, thin tail swished back and forth erratically. The type of creature it was on the tip of Hector's tongue. At last the horn ceased to exist, the vehicle decimated beyond recognition. It lifted its regal, twisted horned head and roared again, vibrating throughout Hector's very bones.

"Dra—dra—dragon!" Hector clapped his hand over his mouth.

The beast turned its reptilian head, glowing amber eyes focusing right on Hector's hiding spot. "That's right," the dragon spoke, its voice smooth compared to its hard exterior. "And where might you be hiding? . . . You reek of death."

Hector bristled then smelled his armpit. He couldn't smell anything. "Have you always been here, dragon?" Worried of being found, he darted to a new spot. Thank goodness he was quick.

The dragon hopped off the demolished junk and strode around, searching for Hector with its nostrils flaring.

Hector made sure to stay on the move, behind things, just out of sight.

"I have been asleep, deep underground here for a long time. Long before this building. Hundreds of years of hibernation, as dragons do. Why don't you come out and show me just what you are?"

"Promise you wont eat me?" Hector risked a peek.

The dragon stood up on its hind legs, eerily resembling a human figure, and made an X with its claws across its breast. "I won't eat you IF you will take me to the nearest village to feast upon its inhabitants."

"The nearest village?" Hector thought about the offer for a minute, about how he didn't even know where he was, then stepped out from behind a rusty tractor. "I guess I could take you out." He glanced down into the pit, at the mutilated car and the corpse inside. "First I need to get rid of this body. Humans are notorious for discovering vampires if we leave our empty snack packs around."

"Vampire? I haven't heard that word in a long time." The dragon lowered itself back onto all fours and walked over, sniffing Hector like a dog. It grimaced. "Bloodsuckers were barely a concern during my time. More like . . . leeches."

Hector shrugged. "Tomato, *tomate*." He knelt, ready to climb down but the dragon's tail whipped in front of him.

"Allow me," it said as a glowing light formed in its throat, and with a rumble, traveled up to its mouth. Five small fireballs hit the car in various places, melting, consuming, destroying everything inside.

Fascinated, Hector could not look away as all the evidence of his crime completely disintegrated into a molten liquid pile. Something else caught his eye; a yellow glimmer just beyond the lip of the crevice. Without drawing too much attention, he leaned forward while scratching his head, peering down. The flames lit up a cavern, full of gold and jewels. A dragon's nest of treasures. If Hector had a beating heart, it would have thumped right out of his chest in excitement. Greed seeped like a slow poison into his veins. His rat race of odd jobs and pickpocketing victims would be over. He could live like a king. With that kind of loot, he could *be* a powerful vampire boss and the others would *have to* respect him.

"Right, let's get you some food," Hector said with new enthusiasm as he straightened. He just needed to befriend the dragon. Wouldn't be too hard, the beast had to be lonely after years of sleeping. "But you need a disguise. People will definitely notice a dragon walking around."

The dragon quirked its head like a curious puppy.

Hector looked around the barn for anything to help integrate a prismatic black dragon into the bland human society then grinned when he spotted just the thing.

)❱●◉◀❰(

"I look ridiculous," grumbled the dragon, fidgeting.

Hector smirked, watching the dragon walk upright like a human beside him down a dirt road. "I don't know. I think you make a great farmer." The denim coveralls he had found fit the dragon perfect—well—near perfect. The back was cramped and bulging, the dragon's tail shoved inside. A straw hat on its head finished the disguise.

A tendril of smoke twirled upwards as the dragon did its best to walk more rigidly, less serpent like. "I am too hungry for this foolishness," it muttered.

They came upon a worn-down, twenty-four hour diner. Its neon lights buzzed in and out of working order. The business had seen better days, probably a long time ago. The aroma of grilled burgers wafted out the cracked back door and the dragon got visibly more pleasant. It clicked its front claws and its long tongue licked at its chops, stomach gurgling in response.

"Shhh, shh." Hector went around the side of the building and peeked at the parking lot. Two lone cars. If he was lucky, the chef and a server. He turned back around and looked at the dragon. "You stay back here. Let me go in and order you some food. I'll bring it out and we can sneak away before the breakfast crowd arrives."

The dragon grumbled, but if it said anything, Hector did not hear as he walked to the front of the diner. He took a deep, meditative breath in and reminded himself that he had already eaten. He could feel his second teeth itching to drop down and the familiar parched-feeling in his throat started to tickle. It had taken him five years since turning to be able to fight against the desire to feast on everyone and everything. Some days were better than others. Bells rang when he opened the door, his meditation done, and he stepped inside.

It was every bit as dingy inside as it was outside. Some of the fluorescent lights flickered, the floor grimy in corners from lack of deep cleaning, and there were duct tape patches in the vinyl booths. Relieved to find the diner empty, he went straight for the counter to order. The server popped up with a handful of ketchup bottles. Distracting silver sparkly earrings swayed back and forth from the motion.

"Oh, hello!" He slid a menu over with his elbow, a million dollar smile upon his face. "Have a seat wherever you like!" Excitement at having a customer rolled off of the server and enveloped Hector.

Way too perky, Hector thought. He was hit with a flashback of another dazzling face wearing long earrings.

"Hi there." She grinned a perfect pearly white smile. Human. A hot human. Talking to him. Hector gulped. "You look . . . thirsty." She produced a wine glass with thick red liquid. He lifted it to his lips, the scent of metallic blood descending his second teeth instantly, and tried his best to only sip it. But she had other plans as she lifted the end of the glass, forcing Hector to chug the blood quicker. It left a funny, numbing feeling in his gums. Unusual, but the woman was hot and she dragged him to the dance floor.

"Yeah, hi," he muttered and kept his head down, looking over the menu. Concentrating on the words rather than the snack in front of him. "I want to order some food to go. How about your famous double burger . . . uh, rare . . ." He realized he didn't know how much a dragon needed to eat or if it even liked its meat cooked or raw. Details he'd find out soon enough. "You know what, two of those. A side of fries and . . . a chocolate milkshake."

Can dragons have chocolate? Or milk? Well, it's not a dog . . . . It probably has eaten some cows back in its day . . . What am I saying? Listen to me! I've got a freaking dragon outside waiting for me!

"So, two Famouses, on the bloody side. Fries. And a chocolate shake—"

"Better make it vanilla!" Hector panic-shouted.

"Sure thing." The server blinked several times then nodded, writing down the order change and disappearing into the back.

Once the server was gone, Hector let out a breath he had intentionally withheld and ran a hand through his hair, thinking about that fuzzy memory.

FIFTEEN MINUTES LATER, the door bells jangled a second time, Hector left the diner with a greasy bag of food and a vanilla milkshake in hand. He walked with a pep in his step, proud of the control he had over his desires, and equally glad that food cost relatively nothing out in the countryside. Maybe he would consider staying there more often.

He found the dragon rummaging in the garbage bin outback and frowned. "Oh, you don't want that junk. Not after you taste what I've got here," he said, holding the bag up. "Come along, let's get back to the barn before the sun comes and leaves me crispy and you exposed."

The dragon let loose steam from its nostrils and dropped the empty cardboard container back into the garbage. "You took too long! I should eat you where you stand," it huffed. It walked beside Hector and poked its nose inside. "However, this does smell a lot better than what I found. And what is that cylinder in your hand?"

Hector cleared his throat, brushing off the threat, and took the lid off the cup. "It's called a milkshake." He removed the lid and offered the cup to the dragon. "People love them with their burgers and fries. Salty, sweet. It's what I liked when I was human."

"Why shake milk? What does that do? Oooh!" The

dragon hummed with appreciation as it dipped its tongue in the creamy, frozen dessert. "Oh. Oh . . . This is truly marvelous. Sweetened milk! And so cold!"

"If you think that's good, try this." Hector dumped a few fries into the shake then held it out expectantly.

The dragon stared, unblinking, at Hector before lowering its jowl into the cup. Swooping the cup up and into the air, the dragon devoured the frozen salty treat. It let out a burp then smacked its lips. "Hmmm . . . Mmm . . . alright, I see the appeal of such a combination. It was delicious despite sounding disgusting." It eyed the bag of burgers. "But I'm ready for that heavenly scented brown paper."

Hector hissed, pulling the bag closer to himself. "First we get to safety."

Bursting out of the coveralls, the dragon grabbed Hector by the shoulders as its leather-like wings unfurled and stretched as far as they could. With a few mighty pumps, they were airborne. Hector panicked, drawing his arms and legs in close, afraid of going splat on the ground. He was fairly sure he could not turn into a bat at will. He had tried it right after his turning. With no success, he assumed it to be either a myth or something older, much older, vampires developed in their personal eternities. The dragon evened out on a pocket of air and set off at a remarkable speed in the direction of the barn, its stomach gurgling as loud as the wind rushing past Hector's ears.

Too terrified to even look, Hector kept his eyes shut tight, clutching the bag of food for dear undead life.

GETTING to the food had taken them the better part of the night. Getting back with the food had taken a mere ten minutes, though Hector preferred walking to flying. He leaned against one of the beams in the barn, willing his stomach to stop lurching as if on a rollercoaster, while the dragon happily ate its burgers and fries. The potential of gold shared by befriending the dragon reminded Hector it was worth it.

"Mmmm," the dragon hummed, then a fiery burp that shook the wood of the building erupted out of it. "That was delightful. Although, much too small for a beast such as I. I am still fairly hungry. Perhaps something more-" —it looked Hector up and down— "-human sized."

The tiny hairs on Hector's neck rose and a chill, his undead body had not experienced before, swept over him. "Something bigger? Really? You are roughly the same size as myself and two burgers would be pushing it, when I was human. Besides . . ." Hector motioned towards the barn door. Soft purple and pink light seeped in through the cracks; dawn was soon approaching. "I can't go out again until evening." He pushed off the beam, hoping the dragon would hold to its deal of not devouring him. "I need to find someplace safe to sleep, away from daylight. Such as . . . a hole, maybe."

The dragon's amber eyes narrowed into slits and it moved closer to the opening in the earth from which it came. "A hole?"

"That is, if you do not mind? It seems the safest place, seeing how you slept there undisturbed for the turn of a century." Hector really did believe that. It was just an added bonus that he could survey the treasure that also lay hidden. "What do you say? You can trust me. I got you that food, didn't I?"

If there were mixed feelings about the proposal, it was not evident on the dark, stoic face of the dragon. Twisting its long neck towards Hector, it grumbled. "I suppose you've proven yourself to some degree. I will allow it, but!" And the dragon stood up tall, wings half spread, a menacing snarl on its face. "If you so much as touch one piece of gold, I'll roast you and devour your insides while you scream beneath my claws."

Hector paused for a moment, picturing himself a vampire-kabob, then shrugged. "Fair enough."

To his dismay, the dragon picked him up by the shoulders once more and hovered over the hole, its claws just starting to pierce his flesh before being unceremoniously dropped. Once the shock wore off, Hector did his best to conceal his excitement. "Aren't you coming down?" he called up to the dragon perched on the edge.

"No," it said, looking away, distracted. "I think I'll keep guard. I've slept much too long. Remember, don't touch anything!" And it disappeared from Hector's sight.

Moments passed and Hector was sure the dragon was gone when he decided to survey the tunnel. He stumbled and slipped down a short slope, crashing into cold, hard metals. The treasure. Fingers spread wide, Hector pushed his hands through coins and gems alike. Relished the clinking noises it made as he dislodged its resting places. As excited as he was, he felt the supernatural tug of sleep and grinned to himself as he curled up atop the dragon's prized possessions. He found a golden crown, the inside blackened a little, and he placed it upon his head before closing his eyes.

Vampire king . . . Has a nice ring to it.

)◗●Ⓜ◀◖(

THE REWARD for sleeping upon treasure was a painful crick in Hector's neck the next evening. He rubbed at the spot tenderly while walking up to the cavern's opening. There was no sign of the dragon, thankfully, and Hector wondered if perhaps with its new freedom the beast had abandoned him, and the spoils.

"At last! You have awakened!" The ground shook from the sheer boom of the dragon's voice. "I am getting very, very hungry!" And it sounded irritated.

Clawing his way up, Hector sighed heavily to himself. "I just fed you, didn't I?" He said as he stood on the upper level and dusted himself off. When he looked up, he was face to face with the dragon, its amber eyes cold and unblinking. Startled, Hector stumbled back, nearly falling into the pit again. The dragon backed away, with a whip of its tail, and circled around to the other side of the pit. As it did, Hector did a double take. He could have sworn the dragon grew a few sizes overnight. But he was too close to really tell.

Something shiny fell from the dragon's claw, down into the darkness of the under level.

"What was that?" Hector thought it looked suspiciously like the earrings the server wore at the diner.

"Nothing, absolutely nothing," it said, then chuckled.

A small inkling of dread formed a pit in Hector's stomach. "Well . . . You know the deal, you'll need the coveralls once we get closer to town."

"Oh, those things? I fear I had an accident and the item was ripped into pieces."

The dread grew.

"No matter." The dragon ducked to step outside and stretched, reaching towards the sky. It had to have grown. "And you *will* find me some food. No need for a silly costume. We will go somewhere else. I do not wish for this . . . diner food . . . you fed me before. I got terrible pangs in my heart."

"I didn't know could dragons get heartburn," Hector remarked and followed. "Say, what's your name anyway?" At once he was accosted by the scent of a fire, stopping him dead in his tracks. Black smoke billowed skywards, blowing in from the direction of the diner. "What . . . what happened while I was sleeping?" he whispered. Whipping around, Hector hurried to catch up to the dragon. "Did anyone see you?"

"You worry too much," the dragon replied as they wandered into a corn field. It plucked an ear of corn off the stalk. "You will put yourself in an early grave." It halted, looked back at Hector, and laughed so heartily that the corn stalks around them swayed with each guffaw the dragon made.

Hector rolled his eyes at the terrible joke and he continued to trudge along. The moon's light was minimal behind dark clouds, so they relied on the near-perfect straight rows to guide them.

"As for my name, a lowly creature such as a vampire would never be able to pronounce it. Mmm. Do you smell that?" The dragon inhaled deeply. "It's sweet. Like honey from bees."

Slowing down, Hector also took a deep breath in. Notes of maple and vanilla floated on the night air, a hint of salty butter following behind. The smell triggered a photograph-like memory, his first meal after coming to America from Mexico. In slideshow-like flashes he saw his mom sitting him in a booster seat, his dad slowly ordering in the foreign-to-them language. And, at last, a stack of golden flapjacks were set in front of him. And although his vampire-body no longer craved such sustenance, there was a sort of longing deep within him. His parents' smiling faces popped forward. He hadn't thought of them in a while.

"Let's keep going." He pushed back the loneliness that the memory provoked. Out of habit, his hand went to his wrist, forgetting the watch he normally wore was still gone. His father's watch. "Someone is making breakfast for dinner. I bet we could convince them to give us a plate."

The dragon clicked its claws excitedly and bounded past Hector, like a rabbit, weaving in and out of the stalks. Hector picked up the pace. "Hey, hey, hey! Wait! You'll be spotted and blow our cover!"

"I care not! I am a dragon! All should cower before me!" The dragon half-roared, half-laughed as it leapt out and onto a manicured lawn.

Hector swore he felt phantom panic-attack pangs in his chest. The unspoken cardinal rule of all 'mythical' creatures was to remain enigmatic, hidden, out of sight. The dragon gave no heed to that way of life. "There's one of you," Hector grunted as he stepped over the dirt berm. "And there's hundreds of thousands of humans in this state alone. Millions on this side of the earth! Please, I'm begging you. Use some discretion."

"Discretion?" The dragon stopped, making Hector bump into it. It twisted its neck around to stare Hector down. "That is not something I understand."

Spooked by the intensity of the dragon's sight upon him, Hector shuddered and avoided making direct eye contact. "Discretion is to keep oneself hidden from view, out of sight, in the shadows."

"I am just so very HUNGRY. I do not care to follow rules, set by *you*, to hide. I want to EAT." The dragon snapped its teeth in Hector's face and steam swirled out of its nostrils. The distinct aroma of fresh human blood wafted out, triggering Hector's vampire senses.

"FINE!" Hector's fangs elongated when he shouted, eyes flashing bright red. "I'll go get you some food but you have to promise to stay put." And without waiting for said promise, Hector darted in the shadows, around a farmhouse. He stepped onto the porch. Every board creaked as he neared the screen door. Not only were there delicious smells coming out, but also a soft humming mingling with a steady flutter of a heartbeat.

"Umm, excuse me?" Hector spoke softly, rapping on the door.

The humming stopped and the sound of house-slippers shuffled towards him. "Who's there?" an older, raspy but feminine voice called out. Her hand rested on the door latch, clearly confused who would call at such an hour of the night, in the middle of nowhere.

Hector stepped into the glow of the yellow kitchen light and smiled sheepishly, careful to keep his fangs concealed. He liked to think he was getting better at tight lipped smiles. "Good evening, ma'am. Sorry it's late, but my car broke down a few miles up the road. I've been walking all evening, looking for a place to call a tow truck." He hoped he looked pitiful, trustworthy, like a grandson maybe.

"Who is it!" A rough voice croaked from farther in the house.

"It's a young man!" the old woman yelled as she opened the door and ushered Hector in. "You poor dear. You look ghastly! Come in, I've just made pancakes and bacon. You can use our phone to call and eat while you wait."

"Oh, but I do not want to impose." Hector stepped over the threshold, its invisible barrier of protection vanishing with her invitation. "I'll just make my call and head back to my car. Again, my apologies for intruding during your dinner."

The kitchen's heat warmed his cold flesh. It was dated, but cute. Mismatched pans hung on a wall, various ladles and spatulas sat in a clay vase on the worn, speckled counter. Bacon sizzled in a well-loved cast-iron pan on a stove probably from the seventies. She flipped the bacon and motioned, with her free hand, towards the wall where a rotary phone hung with an extra-long twirly cord. Hector went over to it, his nerves a little shaky, and fake dialed after thumbing through their aged phone book. He turned away from her, hiding the fact he kept a finger on the cradle to prevent the dial-tone, and muttered about car problems he had heard about in films. What did Hector even know about cars? Nothing! He never had one, he didn't need one living in the big city. Glancing over his shoulder, he made sure the old woman wasn't paying attention, then hung up the phone with a big, fake sigh of relief. "Luckily the tow place was open," he said loud enough this time for her to hear.

"What's the matter with your car?" An old man yelled from the darkened living room. The only light came from a tv that illuminated every crevice and wrinkle on the man's face. A walker sat beside him, but he looked like he hadn't gotten up in a long time.

A news segment came on the tv and Hector strained to listen without being obvious. "I don't, uh, know." He leaned closer to the room. "Steam just started coming out of it."

"The fire that broke out in local favorite BurgerStop, continues to burn on despite firefighters' best efforts, leaving almost nothing left of the iconic diner. Still no traces of either the chef or server from the night shift. If anyone has information on the two or how the fire was started, please contact Woodstock Police Department at—"

He knew it. He just knew it had to be the dragon. Why else wouldn't the firefighters be able to put out the fire? It was dragon fire! The strongest fire *not* known to man. And 'iconic?' Hector had been in graveyards that looked better taken care of than that place.

"Turn that down, Ennis!" The old woman waved her spatula at her husband. "Leave the boy to eat. He looks starved to death. Go back to watching your shows." She picked up a pancake, adding it to a large pile on a serving plate. "Now, you sit down. I'll fix you right up."

Hector smiled at her kindness. His heart might not beat, but there was still a soft spot for grandmas. "Oh, unfortunately I cannot stay. The tow company told me to be ready by the car. But could I trouble you for that lovely stack of pancakes to-go?"

Compassion washed over the woman's face and she nodded. "Of course, dear. How many? Two? Three?" She pulled out a paper plate and put pancakes on it.

Hector cleared his throat, "Um . . . All of them? If it's not too much to ask."

She stared at him for a moment and he worried she'd suspect something was off about him. But then she chuckled to herself and put the heap of pancakes back on the serving tray, instead pulling out plastic wrap, and sealed the steaming cakes up tight.

"And . . . some bacon, if you don't mind," Hector added.

"Of course, honey." The woman laughed.

)◗●◖◉◗●◖(

OUTSIDE, the dragon paced back and forth as Hector made his way down the lawn, the plate of food gripped tight in his hands. From the distance between them he could make out that the dragon was indeed much larger than the first night. Excluding its tail, it was a good foot taller than him, even when standing on all fours. Its belly was more rounded than slender. And he might have imagined their frailty before, but the wings looked thicker, healthier, with an oily sheen to them. When the dragon turned, he noticed a spot behind its front leg was missing some scales and a superficial gash was healing, crusty brown blood around it.

"About time!" The dragon bellowed, moving quickly beside Hector. "Oh, that smells so delicious! Like years of experience and craft."

Hector raised his brow at the comment and handed the plate to the dragon. While the beast consumed, he searched for any other signs of a fight on its long body. Scratches and old scars, but only the one fresh. He looked back at the house and worry for the old couple inside gripped him. A wicked thought formed, both to protect the innocent farmers and to take care of a problem Hector struggled with.

"Listen, dragon."

The dragon had eaten the bacon first and was mid-dropping the pancakes inside its mouth when it looked at him.

"I've thought of another place to take you, for food. Lots of it."

"Ah," the dragon grinned. "Finally. You understand that a mere little *human* meal . . . such as this-" —he held up the plate of pancakes then tipped them into his mouth and swallowed them whole— "-would never satisfy a beast such as myself."

"Sure," Hector nodded. "Right. I can understand that, now. I've just remembered the perfect spot. A place we can *both* be who we are and enjoy those certain meals we desire. Around others like us."

"You don't fit in here, you aren't one of us." Hector's head spun, he tried to form words to tell them he did, but his tongue felt like lead and his eyelids wouldn't stay open.

"Vampire? You were saying?" The dragon nudged Hector out of the flashback.

"Right. But we'd need to fly, to get there quicker, if you didn't mind carrying me again." The more that night came back to him, the more Hector liked his new plan. He wanted to be done with this adventure. Taking on the dragon as a new friend, a sort of pet, had turned out to be more trouble than he thought. The treasure was close in sight.

Movement by the corner of the house caught his eye. Both himself and the dragon zeroed in as the old woman came around. She stopped in her tracks when she saw them, the guy she had so graciously *fed* and a mighty creature beside him. Hector waited for the screaming to start. A glance at the dragon found it grinning wickedly. Instead of screaming, the old woman surprised them both by reaching for a shovel leaned up against the house. Hector backed away. The dragon was not so smart.

With a fierce yell, the old woman ran as fast as her legs would allow, straight towards the dragon. A metallic twang sounded in the night. She whacked him square in the head, a visible rattle throughout its skull and spine. The dragon's eyes crossed and it recoiled away from her like a terrified snake.

A low growl rumbled deep within the dragon.

"No!" Hector yelled, too late.

Swift as a viper, the dragon snapped its jaw around the upper half of the old woman and Hector watched, mortified, as the lower half fell over. The sound of bones grinding between the dragon's teeth loud in his ears. Within a few moments, the dragon scooped up the legs and devoured them too.

Hector couldn't think of anything to say. He was beyond traumatized. It wasn't until the dragon belched that he could even think past the horror.

"You just . . . you ate her. You ate that little old woman."

The dragon looked at Hector curiously, no sign of remorse behind its golden eyes. "Yes, I did," it said simply. "I told you I was hungry."

"Hungry? *Hungry?* I just fed you! The—the—the pancakes and bacon!" Hector pulled at his hair and in pure frustration yelled at the top of his lungs into the night sky.

"Nettie? Are you okay?!" The old man called from inside the house.

"Great, just great." Hector looked towards the house, half expecting the old man to come out with a pitchfork.

The dragon perked up, heading towards the house, up on the deck, and poked its head inside. Hector couldn't be witness to the atrocity and turned his back to the farmhouse. Looking out at the cornfield, he wondered how the night had gone so wrong. Two gunshot blasts startled him and he jerked back around. Who would come out of the farmhouse? A sigh, either of relief or disappointment, he wasn't sure, left him when the black glimmering head of the dragon peeked out first. It had a slight limp as it hopped down from the deck and came to him.

"So," the dragon said, as if nothing had happened. "Where's this place you spoke of?"

"Are you okay?" Hector looked for a gunshot wound but the dragon turned to the side, unfurling its wing as it tilted towards him.

"Just a scratch. Get on." After Hector climbed aboard, the dragon grunted and struggled for a moment to right itself. "Keep your eyes open this time, I don't want to get lost. Try to remain centered and don't let go," it commanded.

With gritted teeth, Hector forced himself to keep his eyes open, as terrifying as it was. The dragon crouched down then leapt into the air. With two powerful pumps of its bat-like wings, they were off the ground. Hector looked down instinctively and whined.

"Hey, focus. Which way?" the dragon growled.

"Oh, right." Hector jerked his head back up. "Southeast thirty miles. Woah! What are you doing!"

"If this *discretion* is your goal, we have to get high above the clouds. Otherwise anyone looking up would see a dragon against the clouds. Get high above them and no one will spot us."

Its wings flapped more, forcing the ground farther down from them. Hector watched as the clouds got closer and closer then all together disappeared. He looked around, wondering where they went, then leaned to the side. Gone was the earth. They soared over puffs of cotton candy. His clothes were damp and he wiped away a thin sheen of moisture from his face.

At last they moved forward. A thrilling sensation like butterflies twirled in a tornado around Hector's belly. They were flying, truly flying, and he was a part of it willingly. The stars were brighter, bigger up there, and they were littered across the sky like glitter on a dance floor. But it was the moon that captured Hector's breath. The great, cold rock glowed pure white light upon him, cleansing him of worry and stress.

"Enjoy the moonlight while you can, vamp," the hot human sneered as Hector faded in and out of consciousness. His head flopped to the side, hitting the car window. They were on a dirt road, rows and rows of corn passing by. When the car stopped, the woman pulled down her mirror and fixed her lip-gloss. "The sun will rise soon. I better get you out before your corpse turns to dust and ruins the leather."

Hector's heavy eyes closed and he fought to reopen them, to make sense of what was happening. He fell forward when the woman opened the car door. The scent of her caused his fangs to tingle and he sunk them into the meaty flesh of her inner thigh. The sounds of her screams seemed far away, drowned out by the rush of fresh blood. He pulled her inside and drank until he couldn't. Still so tired, so disoriented, he slid into the driver seat and started the car. He needed somewhere to shelter before dawn broke. A broken down barn was close by.

The moment was whipped from him when the dragon dipped to one side and Hector nearly lost his balance. He cursed, but forgot his anger when he saw the moon's effect on the dragon's body. The deep black scales swirled with that rainbow prism oil slick from their first meeting, the colors moving and shifting like a kaleidoscope. It was beautiful, hypnotizing. He could watch the multicolors dance along the beast's muscles all night. But a blinking red light ahead of them alerted Hector they were closing in on the city. The tip of a skyscraper a clear marker for the city below. Hector tapped the dragon's side with his heels to indicate they arrived and the dragon started their descent.

Below the clouds, large buildings with hundreds of

windows reflected the dragon spiraling down. Hector guided it towards an alley he knew well. His stomach did a flip when the dragon dropped to the ground. Hector was more than glad to slide off.

"Where is the food you promised?" The dragon growled, turning its head to glare at Hector. "After that flight, I am once again starving. I'd even eat *you*." It snapped its teeth too close to Hector's face, again.

"Stop that!" Hector growled back, taking one step back. He was so done with the dragon's attitude. "Come this way. There should be a subway entrance around this corner. Then you can feast your little heart out."

"Excellent," hissed the dragon and it followed close, breath hot on Hector's neck.

)❭●◉●❬(

THE SUBWAY TUNNELS were devoid of activity, save for a few sleeping humans that made the underground their shelter. Although the stench of many passersby throughout the day lingered. Their discarded trash filled the stairway and clanked around under the dragon's swaying tail, the sound echoing off the grimey tiled walls. Hector sighed when an aluminum can clattered past him. The element of surprise would not be theirs.

He led the dragon down onto the tracks and they walked along in the dark, then into a low, skinny tunnel for some time until at last a red glow lay ahead. Clearing his throat, Hector mentally prepared for what was to happen next. Beside him, the dragon sniffed and grew excited, its stomach gurgling in response.

They rounded a bend and were bathed in the red

lighting as a platform with caution tape came into view. Hector's nerves were in a tight ball as he jumped up and over the tape, gazing around the landing. The dragon was nowhere in sight. A handful of vampires lounged on old subway chairs in one corner, others stood around a trash can fire pit in the center of the room. One of them, in a long trench coat, noticed Hector's arrival and nudged a mohawked vampire next to him. The two that Hector remembered seeing last. He scratched his palms nervously as they left the fire light, heading straight for him.

"What have we got here? Little Hector made his way back, eh?" the trench coat vampire sneered. His friend split away so that they surrounded Hector. "Thought we saw the last of you Saturday night."

"Yeah, well. I'm tougher than I look, I guess." Hector shrugged. He wondered when the dragon would show itself.

The flash of a blade flipping out and the two vampires stepped in closer. "I *thought* we told you we didn't like your kind in our group. You're weak, you're dumb, and you have nothing to offer the clan. You don't fit in," Trench Coat spat.

"*Yeah*," agreed the other. "That's why we drugged you and sent you to die in the middle of nowhere."

Hector wasn't surprised to learn that, he had suspected as much all along, but it still stung to hear. He didn't fit in as a human and he didn't fit in as an immortal blood sucker. Why? Because he was an immigrant? Because he was a fledgling vampire? Or because he had to pickpocket to survive? He clenched his fist, drawing his own blood out of anger. They'd be sorry, they'd all be sorry once they saw him rich as a king off the dragon's treasure. "Then again . . . you won't live long enough to see it," Hector said aloud.

The two paused, face scrunched in confusion. Trench Coat pulled his knife arm back, ready to stab.

With a loud thud, the dragon landed on the platform behind Hector, extended to its full size, wing tips touching the walls in marvelous display. A glowing ball of fire ignited in its opened mouth. It spat the ball onto the vampire in the trench coat, who erupted into shrieks of pain. The other vampires stared in wide-eyed shock.

Darting its head down, the dragon snapped the other vampire in half. Terrified shouts intermixed with the sound of bones snapping between sharp teeth, echoing off the walls. Trench Coat, ablaze, was on the floor pleading for help, but no one came and he, too, was soon snapped in half.

Hector smirked and stepped out of the dragon's way, his arm out in offering towards the rest of the piss-ons. The meal he had promised. He watched, entertained, as the dragon folded up its wings and bound from one area to the next, gobbling up all in sight. Who would have guessed that justice in the form of screams would sound so sweet?

A vampire tried to flee past Hector, but he was quicker and pulled the vamp back by its hair, exposing its neck. He sunk his fangs into the other's neck and drank his fill. He had never fed on his own kind before. It was thrilling, but he was cautious to not get sucked into the bloodlust like the dragon was indulging in. With a vicious rip, Hector pulled away and spat out the flesh. Tossing the bleeding vampire towards the dragon, it caught the body like a dog playing fetch. As it chewed, the dragon looked around. Hector pointed towards a corner filled with shaking boxes, those hidden inside terrified for their lives.

While the dragon played cat and mouse with the last of the vampires, Hector dug in the pockets of the lower halves, taking their money and trinkets. "Ah," he exclaimed, holding up a gold watch in the dark lighting. He flipped it over and ran his thumb over the inscription. *Estar orgulloso.* *"Be proud,"* he repeated in English, slipping his father's watch onto his wrist, back where it belonged. They must have taken it when they left him for dead.

"What's that you've got?"

Hector nearly jumped out of his skin when the dragon poked its head over his shoulder. "Family heirloom, it's all that I have left of them," he said and backed away. It was time to go. He could feel the night slipping away, and he still had another stop before he could rest. His eyes darted to the dragon's swollen belly, hoping his plan would work. "Listen, dragon, I've got to get going."

Alarmed, the dragon sat up straighter and took a heavy step towards Hector. "You mean *we*, surely."

"Ah," Hector half grinned. "Unfortunately . . . no, no I don't mean *we*. You, my big, walking and talking, human eating, cover blowing friend will not be coming." Feeling confident in his calculations, Hector turned his back on the dragon, hopped down to the tracks and towards the exit. A thud shook the ground and he stumbled. Regaining his balance, Hector picked up the pace.

"You will not leave me here!" the dragon yelled while it tried to keep up. "We had a deal! You feed me and I wouldn't eat you!"

Hector shook his head, standing just inside of the dark tunnel. "Ah, but my friend, I have kept my end of the deal. Now I want a better prize. A dragon's hoard of riches."

The dragon released flames of anger out of its nostrils as it barreled down the tracks and crashed into the face of the tunnel. It roared its frustration, attempting to flatten itself to the ground to fit. No use, it was simply too plump. "You have tricked me!"

Sidestepping just out of the dragon's claw reach, Hector smirked. "That I have. And if you behave, I'll send you more snacks that you may eat and keep their treasures for your own. Start a new hoard. Now . . . *adios.*"

With that, Hector left.

Quickly, to avoid being barbecued in retaliation by the dragon's flames that licked at his heels.

"Hey, James."

Hector waved to a broad bouncer standing at a podium, guarding the entrance to the club the clan owned. There was a dumbstruck look on James' face, failing to conceal his astonishment that Hector had survived. "Uh, yeah. Hey, Hector."

"The bosses want me to take over your post for the night, they have a bigger project for you." Lying was getting easier for Hector. He kept eye contact with the guy as he leaned against the podium. "They said to meet them at the hideout. Don't. Keep. Them. Waiting." Hector clapped his hands in the bigger guy's face, which promptly put the other in a frenzy to leave. When the guy disappeared around the corner, Hector chuckled to himself and walked away.

"That takes care of that. You won't be needing these." Pulling the bouncer's keys from a drawer, Hector tossed them in the air then caught them. "This time tomorrow night, I will be the richest vampire in all of New York."

A laugh from deep within bubbled out of him, harder

than he had ever laughed in his adult life. He laughed so hard and crazy, into the moon lit night, that someone in an apartment across the way yelled at him to shut up.

Things were going to be different for him. All because he had tricked a dragon.

THEY'LL MAKE MONSTERS OF US ALL

BY AMANDA STOCKTON

"Do not stray too far, my dear. These woods are not kind. A girl mustn't be alone. Who knows what she may find."

To which, Girl replied, "These woods are my home, sir. I am the wolf, guardian of fear. And you are quite right. I do not take kindly to trespassers here."

In a time when a low-rent woman's only options were to sell her body to the brothel or sell her body to the war . . . Cirisonna chose the war; and, when it came down to it, still got fucked.

Most of her days, for three years, were spent tirelessly sitting in trenches of mud and shit and corpses of her fallen comrades. In a decade-old war that had wrought nothing but suffering for her people. Which, of course, is what war does best. A violent endurance test to see whose people can suffer the longest and claim the title of victor.

Cirisonna was not born a soldier. She hardly considered herself one while brandishing a rifle and donning her country's steely gray uniform. She followed orders, buried her dead friends, and sat watch at the end of the trench-line with an old curmudgeon of a man and mentor. Frank was his name, and it suited him and his relentless need to spill out every cantankerous thought that ever came to his mind. The drinking didn't help.

He slipped a hand under his heavy gray coat and pulled from it a small silver flask. Cirisonna didn't ask what he was drinking. She never did. But a smell similar to kerosene invaded her senses, and she scooted herself to the opposite end of the stump they'd been using for a chair.

"It'll put hair on your chest," Frank said, tightly twisting the cap closed.

"And this is where I remind you, for the dozenth time, that I am a woman."

"Eh, don't give me that shit. Women ought to be twice as hairy as men." He leaned in close and cocked an over-thick gray brow. "Makes ya less slippery."

She grimaced at the heavy scent. "Is that why you never married? Did you catch yourself a big one, and she slipped away back into the Lake of Sorrow, never to be seen again?"

But Frank didn't reply. His pupils had gone dark and wide and all he had left in him was staring into the blank gray sky. The same nothing-gray it had been since Cirisonna arrived at the front lines. Longer.

She'd arrived terrified yet ready to fight for her people, for her land, for justice, for honor and glory. Everything the recruitment posters promised: Chase the Kalandrin invaders—burn their plague from the Lancheon soils— back to their king and be handsomely rewarded for your service in victory. But there was no honor or victory to be found under that damned gray sky. So when Frank would pull the little silver flask from under his coat and drink whatever smuggler's liquor it contained, Cirisonna didn't ask questions. He'd been there practically from the start.

And that line, that trench where they lived and would likely die, hadn't moved. Not an inch.

"Do you think it will ever change?" Cirisonna asked, pulling her own coat close around her body. "That we will ever see the stars again?"

"Why you wanna look up there for?" the old man grumbled. "You busy lookin' up there, you'll miss what's tryin' to kill you down here. So long as that sky stays gray, you stay alive."

"I dunno, Frank, this just doesn't really feel like livin'."

"You're breathin', ain't ya?" Frank picked a stick from the mud and jabbed it at Cirisonna's chest. "Keep that thing beatin' and you'll do okay."

She smiled and dropped her head. "Maybe you're right. Maybe I could go for a drink."

"Nah. There's still hope in you. Wait until the last of the light goes out before you salt and burn the thing that remains."

The two sat in familiar silence amongst the cold until a soft white began falling from the sky.

"Bugger this," Frank spat. "It's close enough to shift change. Marshall and Vance can sit their daft asses in the snow to keep watch over all the nothing." He got up and started walking back to the belly of the trench, Cirisonna close behind.

They got back to their spot, their muddy home, the snow still falling on their heads. Frank took another swig from the flask. He placed it on the shelf he had carved in the trench wall and dug through his trunk.

"Damn cold's locked my fingers up again," he spat and grabbed the flask for another drink. He murmured something scathing under his breath and laughed. When he turned around to where Cirisonna leaned against the wall, he stopped cold. Like he'd forgotten she was there. His eyes flicked from her, down to his trunk, and settled up at his flask. She waited for some criticism or nihilistic comment. But, to her great confusion, Frank offered her the flask instead.

"Didn't you just say not to salt the earth before it's all dead?"

"I say a lot of shit. Take a drink."

She reached for the flask, hesitant, expecting him to pull it away or call her a name. He didn't. He just let her take it.

"Don't smell it. You want to drink it, not fuck it."

The bottom of the flask lifted and a putrid liquid poured into Cirisonna's mouth.

Four months prior, a mortar attack hit a caravan troop on their way to deliver supplies to the trenches. Cirisonna was part of the recovery team they sent out after the shooting stopped. Eight days later. In the humid heat of summer. The mess of gore and rot and puddles of juices that used to be people was a pleasure to her gut compared to whatever the fuck was in that flask. It burned going down her throat and her insides groaned and bubbled with an audible displeasure.

"That's how you know it's working. Hit it again."

Cirisonna's hand, clasping the flask, hung in the air, trying to force it back upon its owner. Frank refused until she obliged his request. Cirisonna forced down another gulp. And this time, after the burning and bubbling, a warmth spread through her chest and out her arms and legs. It erupted in her head, lifting it clear from her body and the war itself.

"Atta girl." Frank pat her on the shoulder, grounding

her back into her body, but she feared she would float away if she didn't hold on.

The two sat, and they drank. The snow fell. And that wonderful warmth provided by Frank's flask turned into a pit inside of Cirisonna. Something so deep and dark she thought it might swallow her up.

"Didn't you ever dream, Frank? Want for something better than . . . this?"

Frank sighed, tucked the flask back in his coat. "There ain't no better, girl. Don't matter if it's here, or back home on Wotten street. It's all of us just fighting for our lives. All we can do is ease the pain, best we can, while we're here."

"I'm pretty sure that's the Wotten Street Brothel slogan." She laughed, but that pit inside Cirisonna widened, just a bit, at Frank's words. How long would it be before she succumbed to that same bitter hopelessness? Where nothing mattered, and despite how hard you try to do something good and right, it will be for nothing. Being afraid, every day of her life, would be for nothing. So, instead, every morning, when Cirisonna would wake, she hoped for a clear-sky sunrise. And every day, it hurt just the same.

She tucked her finger into her coat breast pocket and a reassuring nose nuzzled her knuckle. Luscious, the nowhere-near-a-barn barn mouse, wiped his face in greeting, and crawled up to Cirisonna's shoulder. She gave him a pat on the head. "Good afternoon, Luscious. Would you like to join me for dinner?"

Luscious scurried to his own hole in the wall.

"Guess not." Cirisonna scoffed.

"Don't be fiddlin' with that rodent of yours. Filthy things, them."

"We are all filthy things, Frank." Cirisonna hadn't

meant to say that out loud. But Frank didn't argue. She supposed he wouldn't.

"Shit," Frank swore. "Left my knife in that stump at the watch. I'll be back."

Cirisonna nodded absently.

"Erm." Frank stopped, looked over his shoulder at Cirisonna, and nodded to himself. "I'll leave this here. I suggest you finish what's inside." He placed the flask on his shelf and headed back out to the watch.

The flask shined as gray as that sky over her head. And she hated the flask all the more. Her stomach threatened dual-exiting if she even considered a drink. Cirisonna cringed. A chill raked up the back of her skull. "I'll pass, thanks."

Her head grew heavy, her face lifted toward the sky, and behind closed eyelids, she imagined a warm bed, soft, with dozens of blankets piled high. She would never leave that bed. It would hold her better than any lover could ever hope. A fire burned nearby. Crackling wood and flickering light in this make-believe room. She focused on the warmth. For a split second, Cirisonna had forgotten where she actually was. For one whole second, there was no war. That was before Luscious saw fit to crawl up her hair onto Cirisonna's face.

"Godless rains in hell!" Cirisonna startled, grabbing the mouse off her face. "Luscious. What on earth could be so important that you—"

Luscious stood in her palm. His little hands presented to her: a blue pearl.

Cirisonna had never seen anything so precious in all her life. "Oh, Luscious, that is quite the treasure."

Luscious placed the pearl in Cirisonna's palm and scampered back to her pocket.

"For me?"

The mouse gave the slightest of nods.

There was no way for the creature to know the value of such a gift. One blue pearl could pay a season's rent back home. She wouldn't even have to go home. She could go anywhere with that pearl.

Cirisonna's hand trembled with nervous excitement. The pearl slipped from her sweat-slick grip. It smacked the ground and rolled out of her reach. She chased after it toward Frank's supply and clawed at the freezing mud, grasping that pearl too tightly in her fist. Her fingers ached and knuckles locked.

"Take care of that for me, will you?" she asked Luscious, slipping the pearl next to him in her pocket.

She considered the flask. Another hard gulp and she could go back to that bed feeling closer to it than ever, thanks to a gift from a mouse. She laughed at herself. Maybe that clear sky wasn't so hopeless.

Before Cirisonna could talk herself into taking a drink, a sheet of paper sticking out through a hole in Frank's trunk caught her attention. Not an ordinary piece of paper. This one had the Kalandrin army seal stamped on its letterhead.

Cirisonna checked each direction for prying eyes before reaching out a cautious hand and grabbed the paper. That black mark of enemy forces ignited a terrible spark in her chest.

Reward . . . informant . . . blue pearls.

Blue pearls. The bulge in her jacket pocket felt like a hot lead weight. Her head turned slowly at the figure that appeared in the corner of her eye. Frank's ghostly-white face silently stared back at her. Their eyes locked together, the truth written in the shame smeared across his expression.

One hundred and fifty blue pearls was the price of his loyalty.

In a broken-hearted whisper, Cirisonna shattered the silence between them. "What have you done?"

But Frank turned and ran. Without thinking, Cirisonna bolted after him. Chased him through the trench. Even as Frank collided with fellow soldiers, she did not relent in her pursuit. She couldn't think. She needed to know the whole truth. And somewhere inside of her, she wanted to be wrong. She wanted to imagine the paper and Luscious's pearl were some unholy coincidence. So she chased after a lie to convince herself it was the truth.

They were nearing the edges of the trench. Their watch was just ahead of them. But where did Frank think he was going? Did he really believe he could outrun what he'd done?

It occurred to her, just then, Frank wasn't running to the watch, or even any part of friendly territory. Frank was running toward the Penumbra Forest.

No one goes into that forest. Frank was always the first one to say as much. The fools who did never came back out. At least not completely. Most people believed it to be haunted and full of unimaginable beasts.

Frank running for the forest stopped Cirisonna in her tracks. She called for him. "Frank! It's not too late!"

He stopped, with his breath labored, shoulders buckled, and he turned. A painfully slow movement, slowed even more by his overworked lungs. He nodded, smiled despite himself. "It was too late the moment they sent me here. I'm sorry, girl. But war is dirty business."

"Business? How could you—"

A violent streak of red erupted from Frank's skull. His

jaw fell slack and soon so did the rest of him, collapsing with a thunk and a crunch of snow.

An explosion thundered in the trench behind Cirisonna. Mud and snow and soldiers were reduced to confetti on the battlefield. To play the part of the blast's decrescendo, soldiers—her friends—screamed in agony. But not in fear. There hadn't been time for fear. Not yet. Everything was still.

A man stumbled, blank-faced, from the smoke and debris of the blast. He repeatedly pushed his tongue out, scraping it against his teeth. Then he looked in Cirisonna's direction. His face was split open from jaw to ear and a curtain of blood wept from the wound.

Fear caught up. For it was at that moment when the screaming really started.

Hoards of soldiers ran for the watch, for the forest, for anywhere that wasn't right there. A stampede of desperate men and women rushed toward Cirisonna, who finally caught up with time and ran with them. Until something enormous but unseen slammed into her, tossing her body like a rag doll through the air. She crashed into the unforgiving, frozen earth and rolled down an icy slope until she finally came to a stop, facing that damned gray sky.

Unlike before, Cirisonna didn't have to wait for the fear to catch up. It was everywhere. This time, it was her body that was behind. Though she may have looked peaceful, in her mind she screamed and panicked. And panicked more because her body wouldn't work. Wouldn't breathe. Wouldn't scream. She would just lie there, another silent snowflake, fallen on the battlefield. Until her eyes got heavy and it all just . . . slipped away.

"Frank!" she heard herself scream. But not out loud. A mouthful of snow told her that. His name etched into her mind through the deafening ringing that threatened to split her skull apart. Like Frank's had.

Cirisonna burst upright, onto her feet, and vomited into the thigh-high snow. She wiped her mouth on her sleeve. Everything around her was a soft, silent white. There was no sign of the trench. Of the explosions. Of soldiers from either side. It was all gone. Buried in a gentle grave. Cirisonna counted among the dead.

She searched for any signs of any other survivors. But with the snow that had fallen since the blast . . . ? "When—How?"

The question was less about how long it had been since the blast and more of how likely. How likely was it for her to find a friendly face? How likely was she to survive? No matter how hard she searched for answers, there was nothing to be found against the bitter quiet of that windless afternoon.

Her fingers were numb, tucked under her arms, hugging herself against the cold. Her lips cracked and bled. And that blood froze into a violent lipstick. Frank would have made a brothel joke. A chill grabbed hold of her heart that had nothing to do with the cold.

"What have you done, Frank?" Cirisonna asked the snow. "You killed us all. For what? Pearls?" A thought. She gasped. A hand swung for her front jacket pocket. To her unyielding dismay, her hand went flat against her chest. Luscious and her blue pearl were gone.

Cirisonna laughed. It was all she had left to her; a laugh of broken edges. So when it burst from her throat, it cut its way out. And a pain she wasn't expecting caught up. And it ripped her apart from the inside. Her jagged laugh crumbled into hushed cries. Even her tears, falling on her palms, hurt.

The tears didn't last. Somewhere along the way, the well went dry. The pain went numb. A ringing in her head replaced the silence of the snow.

"Are you out there?" a man's voice called out.

Cirisonna's heart nearly leapt out of her throat.

"We're here to help," the man called again.

Cirisonna dropped back into her snowy would-be grave. He called out again. Waited for her to give herself away. But Cirisonna would not oblige them based on some elementary promise of salvation.

"H-here!"

Cirisonna clasped a hand to her mouth. She knew that voice. It was distant and her teeth chattered, but Cirisonna had no doubts that it was Kalina's voice. She'd only arrived to the trench a few months prior. Her father had sold her to the army to pay off his drinking debts. She cried herself to sleep every night.

"Here!" Kalina called out again.

"Shit," Cirisonna whispered. It was possible the men were friendly. But it was just as likely they were Kalandrin troops. If not more so.

"It's good we found you," the man said.

"I w-want to go home," Kalina stammered.

"Have you seen anyone else?"

Cirisonna peeked over the snow. A good hundred yards away, a dark-haired man in a black uniform stood between her and Kalina. Two more Kalandrin soldiers approached Kalina. One blond man and one red-haired woman.

"No. I haven't—I haven't looked. You're the f-first people I've s-seen since the blasting started."

"Good," said the man standing before her.

"Good?"

"Makes our job easier."

The blond-haired man leapt and swung. A thunk and a squish later, Kalina was on her knees, an ax buried in her skull.

Cirisonna ducked and laid back down in the snow. Her chest heaved with panicked breath. Of all the things she imagined coming along to kill her, she did not expect the Huntsmen.

Known to be brutal, relentless killers, trackers, and overall really fucking scary, the Huntsmen were a Kalandrin cleaning crew. No survivors, no witnesses. Frank sold out the line, and the old fool really believed they would just let him walk away.

A cloud of white wafted up from her hiding spot with each anxious exhalation. Taking a deep breath, she slowly rolled onto her belly and shoved a handful of snow into her mouth. The next exhale yielded no white flag of fog. She breathed a little easier, but waited for a knife in her back just the same. Cirisonna reached to her leg, where her own knife was strapped, and freed it from its sheath. Numb fingers gripped the blade, held it close, ready should she get the chance to react.

React? Against the Huntsmen? As if she stood any chance in a fight with one of them, let alone three.

"It's cold as piss out here." A man's voice she didn't recognize. Closer to her than Kalina had been.

Cirisonna held her breath. There was no telling exactly where the man was or which direction he faced. But he was close. The snow shifted under his gait and Cirisonna desperately tried to hear which direction he was going. But the damn ringing in her ears drowned out the sound the harder she tried to listen. Or maybe he was moving away. Cirisonna knew it would come down to it, eventually. They would find her, or the freeze would, or whatever monsters might be lurking in the forest would come out to feast at the buffet of her dead friends.

She pushed herself up, just above the snowline. The Huntsman stood ten yards off. He wasn't one of the men Cirisonna had seen kill Kalina. This fourth Huntsman was about her height, based on how the snow met his thighs. His hair was shaggy and brown and he twirled an ax in his right hand.

Cirisonna got her feet under her, matching her movements to his, to mask the snow crunching underfoot. With no sight of the other three Huntsmen, she crept forward. Keeping low, her shoulders barely above the snow, Cirisonna closed the gap between herself and the man sent to kill her.

He stopped.

Cirisonna crouched lower.

He flicked his wrist; the ax twisted around and caught back in his grip.

Cirisonna sat back on her haunches, ready to leap.

The Huntsman's head turned downward. He crouched, plucked something from the snow with his free hand. "Hello, beauty."

Cirisonna's heart all but stopped. She kept low, still, quiet. If he knew she was there, he didn't act like it. He didn't turn, or attack, or acknowledge her in any way. What he did do was hold up a singular blue pearl between his fingers. Cirisonna's blue pearl.

She took advantage of the perfect opportunity of distraction and leapt. Her knife found purchase in the Huntsman's back. He groaned as air was forced from his lungs. The knife tore from his flesh and painted the snow. Before Cirisonna could get the blade in again, he turned, inspected her inquisitively. As though she were some unknown creature, spawned from the snow itself. In a way, she was exactly that. For even Cirisonna didn't know what she would do then. The two of them locked eyes, knowing only one would see nightfall; the second felt like an eternity of uncertainty.

Ax and knife raised and clashed and fell without tasting flesh. The two soldiers fell into the snow, the Huntsman on top of Cirisonna. The blade of his ax poised for her head. His free hand held her wrist that gripped her knife, pinned it into the frozen earth. Cirisonna's other hand trembled with the burden of keeping that ax, and the weight of that man, from bearing down, and making Kalina's fate her own.

"You're a frisky one. I like that." He spat as he spoke. But he screamed when the heel of Cirisonna's boot hammered down onto his open wound. The man lurched, his back arched, and Cirisonna used both feet to kick him in the chest and off of her.

She scrambled over him but threw herself back when he swung the ax toward her middle. Stabbing downward with a reverse grip on her blade, Cirisonna's knife planted into the Huntsman's bicep. Her opposite boot crashed down on his wrist. If it was the ice or his bone that crunched on impact, she couldn't tell. But he screamed again.

She yanked on the blade against his thrashing, and the steel snapped off in his bone. The Huntsman erratically swung the ax once more, with far less strength and precision. Its blade grazed Cirisonna's jaw. A bite of pain seared her skin, but she remained intact.

The ax fell from the Huntsman's grip, landing in the snow with a gentle grace while his other hand rounded up in a fist and clobbered Cirisonna in the cheek. She rolled off of him and he was on her again. His hands wrapped around her throat. A spark of rage in his eyes longed to bleed the life from her. She stabbed her broken blade into his collarbone with one hand. And the other gripped the discarded ax.

She bit her lip in emphatic rebellion, and spat out, "Fuck you." She swung the ax and planted it firmly in the Huntsman's temple. His face twitched, and he clumsily poked at his own weapon lodged in his skull, confused and empty-eyed.

He fell to the side, dislodging her knife as he went. Exasperated, Cirisonna sat up, and watched the man's body for any signs of life. Instead, she heard a woman scream.

A red-haired Huntsman woman looked down upon Cirisonna, fifty yards up the trench hill. She screamed again, a feral fury of despair, and called for her companions.

Wasting no time, Cirisonna turned and ran the only direction she could: toward the Penumbra Forest. She fought against the deep snow and her burning lungs for the trees that disappeared into darkness. Possibly trading one death for another. But it was the only chance she had.

Luckily, the same snow that slowed her also slowed the Huntsmen.

"She killed Alec!" the red-haired woman yelled. "Shoot her!"

Cirisonna fixed her eyes upon the shadows behind the trees and did not slow or look back. A gunshot cracked and a red mist clouded the surrounding air. She felt nothing but her lungs burning and her heart thunderous in her chest.

"You got her!" one of the men shouted.

"Drop her!" the woman demanded. Another shot cracked through the air, but there was no red mist to paint the winter with her death.

There were the trees. Cirisonna gasped with the final

few steps it took to cross their threshold. The trees were dark and tall and bare. Shadows patched the spaces in between. And though she couldn't explain it, she knew there was something lurking within those dark places. Something with eyes that pierced her heart.

A dizzying euphoria swelled in Cirisonna's mind. Her feet would no longer carry her forward. Despite every effort on her part to move, something held her in place. She stood, a silent vigil to her own death on the outside. Inside, she was screaming. But the screams made no sense. They were not hers; not her thoughts, not her voice. They were echoes of screams, of howling and the cawing of crows.

The world around her spun into a heavy, black nothingness, until the screams in her head went suddenly silent. Not because they left her. But because something bigger and more commanding seeped in. It overwhelmed her senses. Sight and sound flickered in and out from blinding and deafening to empty silence. A tear fell down Cirisonna's cheek. The salt of it burned the cut left by the Huntsman's ax, telling her she was still alive. Then, the invading force crowded her face, snuffing out the air. And in her head, a singular, unknown voice whispered, "Mind the path."

)◗●Ⓜ◖◖(

"Mind the path!" Cirisonna's own voice echoed in her ears, both a whisper and a scream, a plea to the forest itself.

She collapsed to her hands and knees in the dirt. Dirt. Not snow, not ice. The dry ground. Solid, unfrozen earth in a strip that stretched far beyond Cirisonna and barely twice as wide as her. Somehow, she'd fallen on a path in the middle of the Penumbra Forest.

There was no sky through the canopy of the trees, their tops hidden somewhere in the forever. Widely spaced, old-growth stood in audience. Their bark and branches creaked as they convened over her presence. The shadows that lurked in between were full of eyes much too large to belong to people. But it was the trees that made Cirisonna's blood run cold.

She winced. The bullet wound finally made its angry presence known with a sharp explosion of pain in her left side. Luckily, it wasn't major. A broken rib or two. Not much blood. She pressed her hand against it and searched her options.

One more time, she told herself. Get up one more time. And she did. She pressed herself back to her feet and took a step. Then another. Following the path. It didn't matter much where it would take her. In truth, she didn't care. Home or Kalandrin territory, she walked one reluctant step after another.

After not more than eight steps, the path was gone. The same path that had just a moment before stretched long and into the shadow simply stopped.

"Okay," Cirisonna said to herself, or perhaps to the trees. She pivoted around to follow the path in the other direction. And it ended, again. "How do you keep to a path that does not keep to itself?"

The forest floor was untouched by the greed of expansion or the brutality of war. Not a thing existed in that place that did not belong there. None except her. And she could feel the trees laying their judgment.

Shaking her head, Cirisonna told herself they were just trees. "Like any other normal tree. That grows in dark, haunted forests, full of unimaginable beasts. And no living survivors to tell their tales." Drawing a deep breath, she stepped off the nowhere path and pressed her palm against the nearest tree. "It's just a tree."

Rough, flaky bark looked and felt just as any other tree. Pinpricks of sap swelled in the pores of the wood. Nothing supernatural. Just a tree. She closed her eyes and rested her head on the bark. A faint chill slowly drifted down her back, and she smiled. She could stand and sway and reach for the heavens. With the wind in her hair and her boots planted firmly in the earth, she could be free, she could be safe. She could be the forest.

With eyes kept shut, Cirisonna recited a folklore:

"What is the shadow in the dark?
    Where goes a path
    Where none dare walk?
    What whispers in the silence,
    When no one speaks or breathes?
    More importantly, I ask,
    Why it is, I do not scream?
    When my flesh turns to bark,
    And the forest is me."

Cirisonna opened her eyes to woody vines growing up her legs. They slithered and coiled around her ankles, rooting her to the earth. She clawed at the slithering flora. But the vines were stronger than her fingers. And the more she fought them, the tighter their grip became. Blood ballooned in her feet and she fell on her backside. She growled, clenched her jaw against the pain of pressure. Her fingers dug around the narrow body of the vines. A glint of silver caught her eye. In the patch of path, her broken knife lay in the dirt.

Cirisonna threw herself toward the blade which had landed just out of reach. She stretched out her arms and struggled to kick her feet, inching closer to the weapon. But the vines moved faster and held her tighter as they crept to her hips. She pounded her fingers into the earth, creating handholds to pull herself closer to the lost knife.

Reaching the blade, Cirisonna released her grip on the earth and wrapped her hand around the metal. The vines jerked her away from the path and stiffened around her legs, forcing her vertical. She hacked at the vines with her knife. The vines pulled and twisted where Cirisonna attacked. Relentlessly, she continued her assault. Even when the vines loosened and writhed, Cirisonna chopped. One end of the vine speared through the flesh of her calf, behind the bone, and out the other side.

She wedged the broken blade between her leg and the vine, and wrenched. It cut through her pants and into her skin as the blade fought against the tough flesh of the vine. She pulled harder on the knife's grip, screamed with fury and agony through her teeth. The vine snapped and flailed, and released Cirisonna before it withdrew back under the ground.

"Shut up, ya twat." Cirisonna recognized the voice of the man who'd found Kalina. The Huntsmen had caught up with her. She scampered quickly behind a tree.

"This place is cursed, I'm tellin' ya," the other man said.

"And I'm tellin' you, shut up. What? What are you pointing at?"

The woman Huntsman replied, "The Path, it ends right here."

Cirisonna dug her fingers into her cheeks to keep her breathing quiet.

"The hell is this?" the first man said.

"It looks like—" The blond was cut off mid-sentence.

Cirisonna pressed herself harder against the tree and her leg burned in protest. Blood bloomed and spilled from her wounds, leaving a trail behind her. She mouthed an expletive. Before her, a path between the trees that hadn't been there before once again vanished when she blinked her eyes.

"She's been here," said the woman Huntsman. Cirisonna couldn't tell just where each of them was, but she knew they were closer now. Too close for her to run. Too close for her to not run. She stared at her blood streaking the ground. She'd barely gotten away the last time she faced just one Huntsman. And now, she had no knife, not even a broken one.

Someone clicked their tongue from the other side of the tree.

Cirisonna tried to find a way out, a way forward, through the trees. But the woods replied to her unspoken plea with nothingness. Not even those eyes from the shadows looked upon her now. Her breath trapped in her chest, her ears strained to hear movement, to indicate how much time she had left.

She pressed a hand into the wound in her calf. Sitting there, waiting for them to find her, to tear her apart, wasn't doing her any favors. If this was to be her last moment, she would at least make them work for it. Using the tree as a springboard, Cirisonna shot up and made a run for it. Her leg wanted to give out from under her, but she refused it. She grit her teeth and hobbled forward as quickly as she could.

"There!"

Her gait hastened at the sounds of footsteps cracking into the earth behind her. Just one moment, one thought too many, and a hand caught her in the back. She fell into the snow. The snow that wasn't there before. On her belly in the ice, Cirisonna waited for hell to find her, drag her away. Boots crunched in the snow on either side of her. One foot on each side.

"No more running, you little bitch."

Cirisonna let out a breath. She screamed and threw her elbow with the full weight of her body into the man's ankle. He dropped to the side, and she scrambled on top of him. Beat his face with with her fists. *Crunch.* He groaned when her punch broke his nose, his blond hair dyed red with his own blood. She didn't relent. Blood gushed from his face. He grabbed her hands and held them in place, keeping her from striking or getting away.

But Cirisonna had teeth. And she used them. She snapped her jaw around his knuckles and ripped her head to and fro like a mad dog. Her mouth filled with blood. Something hit her from behind. When she fell off the Huntsman, she took his finger with her.

"She bit off my fucking finger!"

Cirisonna spit out the amputated digit and laughed while foreign blood drained down her cheek.

"You think this is funny?" the blond Huntsman yelled, cradling his bloodied hand.

"Be quiet, Victor."

"Barent, she killed Alec," the woman hissed.

"She bit off my fucking finger!" Victor yelled again.

"Shut up about the goddamn finger. My brother is dead!"

The dark-haired man—Barent, the woman called him

—looked down upon Cirisonna with an empty inquisition. Ragged breath ripped from her chest, but her eyes stayed fixed upon Barent. The other two would not make a move without his allowance. He knelt down beside her, grabbed her chin. Cirisonna jerked away, but he dug his fingers into her face and forced her obedience.

"You've proven to be quite tedious. I loathe tedium," he said, his voice low and dark. Barent stood back up, looked at the other two, gave an ever so slight nod of his head, and wiped his hands.

The woman was on her first. She stomped on Cirisonna's stomach, on her ribs. Her chest. Cirisonna gasped for air when an audible crack resounded from her middle. Victor, still holding his broken hand, stomped on Cirisonna's hand, ground her fingers under the heel of his boot. Cirisonna howled with pain. Victor lifted his boot and Cirisonna rolled over onto her belly, trembling, and tried to crawl away. A kick to her belly made her futile escape attempt short. They kicked her so hard her body lifted from the ground. Another blow to her ribs and she rolled again onto her back.

She gulped on something pooling in her mouth. Her eyes focused again and caught sight of the glittering sky. The moon, full and bright, gleamed above her like a beacon of welcome from the heavens.

A boot cracked into her mouth, her lips split apart in a violent bloom of flesh and teeth. An array of red painted a halo of blood in the snow.

The woman climbed on top of Cirisonna and wrapped her hands around her throat. "You should have just died back in the trench. Why wouldn't you just die?"

Cirisonna weakly clawed at the fingers knitting away her breath. She reached out a hand for the Huntsman's face, her eyes. But the woman was too tall and Cirisonna too wounded, fading from the world. Those hands held firm on her throat. The air wouldn't come. There was no more fight left in her.

The stars fell around Cirisonna in a blanket, an astral sarcophagus coming to take her away. Someplace where that moon shone through a clear glassy sky and warmed her broken body.

"What are you doing?" a little girl's voice calmly asked.

The hands on Cirisonna's neck loosened, as all the Huntsmen startled at the sudden appearance of a small girl with long black hair, barefoot, wearing a nightgown. Her face was void of expression despite the violence set before her.

Cirisonna gasped for air. Her lungs ached with the want of it. She choked and heaved. The world spun, and the stars ascended without her.

"Where'd you come from, little girl?" the woman asked, rising up off Cirisonna. "Don't you know it's dangerous in these woods?"

"Yeah, these woods is haunted," Victor chided.

Barent lowered himself to her level. "Are you lost?"

The little girl looked down at Cirisonna bleeding in the snow. She raised an eyebrow. "These woods are my home, sir." Her gaze shifted from Cirisonna to Victor, who broke into laughter. The Huntsmen regarded one another with snide smiles spread wide on all their faces. A growling flash of crimson and Barent was gone. Out of sight. The other two barely moved or made a sound to indicate they'd even seen what happened. And then Barent's body smashed down into the ground at Victor's feet. Their leader had become nothing more than an unrecognizable hunk of twisted, dead flesh.

The remaining two Huntsmen stood mouths agape and wide-eyed at what remained of Barent. A sorrowful whimper thought to slip through the red-haired woman's mouth, but a blur of black ripped her away from the earth. Her ensuing scream faded away on her sudden ascent into the canopy of the forest. Victor haplessly fired his gun into the trees. "What are you?!"

The not-little-girl had become something else. She was tall and faceless, with long black hair and fang-like teeth that shone like stars in a black sky. Her fingers formed long claws that stuck out from white robes. She wrapped her hand around Victor's throat, whose toes lifted from the earth.

"What big eyes you have." The creature spoke in a voice not of the child it pretended to be, but in a corrupted, twisted version of it. The sound was bitter in Cirisonna's ears and that cold sank into her heart in a way that made her certain she would never feel hope again. "Do you see me now, boy?"

Victor groaned in reply.

The creature smiled a terrifyingly wide grin. It clenched its fist and, with a crunch and a pop, Victor's body collapsed into a crimson pool in the snow. His head, rolled to Cirisonna's feet.

The creature turned its attention, once again, to Cirisonna and flicked Victor's blood from its claws. A pair of black orbs that shone like wolves' eyes examined her state of finality. When the creature loomed over her broken figure, a weak gasp of air pulled at her failing lungs.

"Tsk, tsk, tsk," it clicked its tongue. "This does not appear well for you, Cirisonna." The voice creaked like floorboards and seared Cirisonna's ears like hot iron. She ached to press her ears into the snow, if only to quench the burning. "You are dying." It drew a long, deep breath, raking its eyes across her purpling body. "And you have been chosen."

Cirisonna's brow furrowed. She tried, despite herself, to choke out the question. "Ch-ch—" She gnawed on the word before she pushed it through her teeth. "Chosen?"

The creature hummed, turned round her hand, and presented Cirisonna with a gift. Luscious, the nowhere-near-a-barn barn mouse, scampered off the creature's claws and onto Cirisonna's chest. He pressed his little hands on her jaw before turning round and crawling into her front jacket pocket.

Cirisonna's mouth twitched into a painful smile, knowing her friend was safe. And what a comfort it was to not die alone.

The creature shoved a finger into Cirisonna's open mouth. Finger, not claw. "What fine teeth you have."

The creature wasn't a creature anymore. Nor was she a human. Hair wafted around her like a cloud of gray smoke that shimmered beneath the moonlight. She leaned in close, black lips grazing Cirisonna's cheek, and inhaled. Their eyes met, locked together. And no matter how much Cirisonna thought to try, she couldn't—or perhaps wouldn't—look away from those nebulous, glassy eyes that shifted in the light. Her skin did the same. In shadow, it was black with whispers of blue and purple. In the light, though, her skin didn't look like skin, but powder. As if a breeze could come along and dust the woods with her. A dark fairy; keeper of the woods.

The fairy pressed a finger into a wound on Cirisonna's scalp. It hurt, but not like it should have. Nothing really hurt anymore. All of her pain, all of her pleasure, every feeling she ever had was a stain in the snow.

The fairy tasted the blood on her finger, grinned, nodded. "It was Luscious who chose you first. The forest agreed." She indicated the hole in Cirisonna's calf. "They wish to welcome you as one of their siblings. I wasn't sure why until now."

She inspected Cirisonna's body closely. "Your war has raged for years. Pushing closer against the walls of my forest. Lives to which I am a shepherd are dying." She craned her head toward the dead Huntsmen. "Your enemies have sown the most death upon the forest." Vines, similar to the ones that had attacked Cirisonna, rose from the soil and wrapped around the corpses of the Huntsmen, pulling them into the earth. "And now their corpses shall feed my wards."

Her hands graced Cirisonna's cheek. Comfort seeped from her touch and Cirisonna yearned for her to keep touching her so long as it mended the pain.

"Mind the path," the fairy whispered. "I can taste it in you. So pure. So full of rage. Trapped. Even while at war." The fairy wiped tears from Cirisonna's eyes and continued. "Do not be afraid. Your life as you have known it is already over. What comes next is entirely up to you. You can continue here, finish your dance with death and feed the trees, become part of the forest." Her hands framed Cirisonna's face, held it gently. "Or you can become rage and put an end to this war."

Confusion knit Cirisonna's brows.

The fairy offered an ethereal chuckle in reply. "I will grant you transformation under this moon that will come with strength unlike any you have ever known. Speed. Agility. You will become a weapon of the forest. My sword of tooth and claw to wreak vengeance and protect my flock."

The question echoed in Cirisonna's mind, *Why me?*

"Your vengeance is my vengeance. Your heart, my heart. Alignment that sleeps in the blood. Sometimes you have to die to find it. And you are dying. So very nearly there, now." The fairy's grip on Cirisonna's face tightened. Her tone shifted in the dark. "But. Should you agree to be my sword, you must end this war and take the Kalandrin throne. Tonight, by the stroke of midnight. Before the full moon recedes."

How? Cirisonna asked without asking.

"Just give me your name, and it will be done. No. You must speak it. You have one breath left to do so."

The fairy leaned in and Cirisonna's eyes took in the light of the moon as she whispered her name in consent.

Darkness took its hold. Crept up her fingers, her hands, wrists. Up her arms. Into her skull. Cirisonna screamed of fire and agony. Her body writhed as it fought against the trespasser coursing through her veins and seeping into her bones, splitting her apart. The full moon reflected in her eyes until there was no light, only the trees in the dark.

And Cirisonna's screams.

Her body twisted, and sinew snapped. And the trees mocked her pain by snapping branches, despite a very obvious lack of wind.

Luscious popped out of her pocket. His tiny body contorted in the air. Black feathers exploded out of his skin. A beak from his nose. Wings and talons from his feet. Luscious the crow cawed and flew away into the trees.

Cirisonna wailed. A hopeless agony ripped from her lungs as limbs popped out of place. Her fingers dug into the earth, desperate for something to hold on to. Until she gave into the tiny pull, hot in her belly. And with nothing more, the world around her was gone.

No more pain.

No more woods.

Nothingness embraced her in a warm blanket of peace.

She opened her eyes and there was light. Brilliant blue light cascaded down upon her face. She dared to smile. For what grace the moonlight suddenly was. As if she'd never seen it before. As if she'd never see it again.

A voice broke through the euphoria. "You have until midnight to end this war and take that throne."

"But it's so far." The sound that came from Cirisonna's mouth was distorted and monstrous. She grasped at her mouth, but what came toward her face were two incredible sets of claws met at the wrist by plush black fur over long, brawny arms and a broad muscular chest. And her face. Her clawed fingers made their way across an elongated jaw full of sharpened teeth. It should have broken her. But at the moment Cirisonna came to find herself to be a wolf, a hidden satisfaction burned inside her where fear once occupied.

"Hold where you want to go in your mind. And mind the path," the fairy's disembodied voice whispered in the dark.

Cirisonna closed her eyes and focused on the Kalandrin castle. When she opened them again, a path had formed beneath her feet and stretched as far south as she could see. A jagged, toothy smile spread across her face. Her clawed hands hit the earth, and she stretched her neck, releasing a thunderous howl from her jaws.

"Go now," called the fairy.

And she did. Cirisonna ran. Four legs moving in rhythm with one another. Claws sank into the earth and pulled her body forward. Hind legs pushed off the ground with such force, sediment kicked up in her wake.

The path wound this way and that. Luscious the crow took the lead, cawing directions and herding the trees. The breeze flowed through Cirisonna's fur and for the first time in her life, she tasted freedom. Even under the contract with the fairy, Cirisonna was more free than she'd ever been while living under her father's roof or as a soldier. She was more than a soldier now. Cirisonna had become the fairy's rage, its vengeance. And in doing so, unlocked her own.

Power and strength coursed through her veins as fear and doubt hardly remained as memory. She couldn't even fathom a reason to be afraid anymore. Except, perhaps, what might happen should she fail the fairy's task.

The tree line broke apart like drawing curtains and there it was: the Kalandrin castle. Black, lean, and tall, the castle was built of jagged stone that never met at the right angle. Spires of iron donned red flags at their tips that flapped in the breeze. Hundreds of miles traveled in a matter of minutes. Was it her new form or another secret of the forest that carried her so far so quickly?

She'd come out of the woods at the castle gardens. Torches lit the path like arms stretched out to welcome her in from the night. She would oblige the gesture.

A lone guard exited the doorway. Cirisonna circled around the torchlight, stuck to the shadows. One massive foot placed round the other, she moved in near silence through the garden, toward the castle and the guard.

Just outside the bounds of the torchlight, Cirisonna crouched and waited as the torch-wielding guard unknowingly moved closer to her. It was the glow of her eyes that he saw first. He stood, free hand on the hilt of his sword, staring at her eyes, trying to make out what he was looking at. Slowly, he moved closer. Cirisonna stood to her fullest extension on her hind legs.

The guard dropped his torch and pulled his sword from its scabbard. The sterling blade trembled in its owner's nervous grip. Cirisonna basked in his fear. No one had ever looked at her in fear before, least of all a man. A fire in her belly erupted at the surge of power that coursed through her. A grin pulled back at the corners of her mouth, exposing her many sharp teeth. That fire in her burned into a low growl.

Before the guard could make a sound, Cirisonna's massive clawed hand wrapped around his neck. He flailed in her grip, futilely thrashed his sword around her ribs, her arm, her throat. But he couldn't do much when Cirisonna clenched her fingers into a squelching fist. His eyes gawked at her until their pupils went wide. Cirisonna watched just a little longer, studying the transition from life to death. And she felt nothing but fire.

She unfurled her fingers, and the dead man collapsed with a thud at her feet. Stepping over him, Cirisonna walked into the light. The toothless maw of the castle shuddered as she ducked her head into the doorway.

It wasn't long before more black-clad guards armed with rifles and swords flooded the hallway. The men in front dropped to their knees and aimed their rifles at the great black wolf standing twice as tall as any of them. Three more rows of guards lined up behind the first. Each of the eighteen men pointed their rifles at her. Their weapons held confidently, but their eyes betrayed them. There, with all of them fixed upon her, their eyes screamed of fear; wide and unblinking. And deeper inside each of their chests, their hearts raced.

Cirisonna jumped at the wall to her left, sprung off of it, and landed in the center of the guards. Her jaws ripped and her claws tore through flesh and bone. Gunfire echoed down the stony hallways, as did the screams of men.

A guard retreated down the hall, his boots splashing in the carnage. Before he reached the corner around which more of his brethren awaited, Cirisonna caught him. He screamed, crunched. Went silent.

In rhythm with the silence, Cirisonna moved swiftly and hurled a corpse at the men in position around the corner. A few fired their weapons. Others yelled profanities. But true silence soon fell upon the halls. And there, Cirisonna found herself before the throne room.

The gilded doors were locked, barricaded, and—Cirisonna pressed an ear against the cool door—a litany of men stood on the other side. One amongst them stood out above the others. One less terrified. *The King,* she thought. *Arrogant fool.*

The door stayed when she beat her fists against it. The door stayed when she launched her body against it. When she clawed at it, kicked it, beat it with a dead body, the door stayed.

The wolf howled.

That heartbeat remained steady.

Cirisonna backed away from the door. The hall before the throne room was purposefully too small for a ram to get enough leverage. But Cirisonna didn't need a battering ram. She backed against the wall, got on all fours, and her feet pushed, launching her against the throne room doors.

The gilded doors cracked open and quickly slammed shut.

The steady heartbeat skipped.

Cirisonna backed against the wall and launched herself once more. The barricade splintered, and the doors burst open.

Without much of a fight, the rest of the king's guards fell. Aside from the mess she'd made on the floor, the room was quite plain. The ceiling rose into a dome, at the top of which a circular window let in the moonlight. More importantly, up a few steps, stood the throne. Abdicated.

But for that last heartbeat, sounding from behind the throne's velvet back, Cirisonna grinned. To end the war–to be finally free–nothing could stop her. She climbed on the throne, peered over its top and dropped a disembodied heart on the lap of the quivering Kalandrin King.

"Your cowardly heart has betrayed you, King Emondon. It is time to pay for your crimes."

"Mercy!" the trembling king begged.

"That is not for me to decide, Your Grace. It is for those you will meet in The Death Marches."

The king cried out for mercy one last time before he fell to the judgment of those he'd condemned to death with his war. And then it was quiet. Nothing but the sounds of her own breathing echoed in the chamber. It was ragged and cruel. And in the quiet, for just a moment, she was relieved it was done.

Cirisonna's appreciation of victory didn't last very long, however. Soon, hurried footsteps rushed toward the throne room. And in through the doors burst a handsome prince. His golden hair framed a strong jaw and piercing blue eyes. Broad shouldered, the prince carried with him a double-sided ax and a shield of silver. He was tall and strong by the looks of his arms. Clearly, a man familiar with battle and death, judging by his reserved reaction to the carnage littering the floor. Cirisonna sat upon his father's throne, unimpressed.

The prince's controlled and steady demeanor took a turn once his eyes settled upon the wolf in his father's seat.

Eyes widened, and his ax shifted in his grip, defensively. The only word he could mutter fell from his mouth like hot iron. "Monster!"

"Monster?" Cirisonna rolled the word around on her tongue, tasting every syllable. It was funny to her, then. That word, so subjective. She supposed, to the prince, she was a monster. Just as his father had been one to her and her people. Where the prince and the soldiers that lie dead at his feet considered him a hero. Cirisonna's great fanged mouth spread wide in a terrifying smile as she accepted the title. "Monster." She practically purred the word, salivating at the notion that she could be his monster. His nightmare. His end.

The prince raised his ax. "I demand you remove yourself from my father's throne."

"Your father has—let's say—rescinded his throne unto me."

"Rescinded?"

"As in, I ate him and took it."

"Lies!" There it was. His heart quickened. He knew what she said to be true. He knew but he couldn't, because it would destroy him.

"Am I lying? What was it your father called my people? Mad dogs? He has reaped what he sowed." Cirisonna stood upright from the throne. Her teeth gnashed as a growl boiled in her throat. "Feast upon your harvest!"

"Every warning of threat and disgrace my father ever spoke about your kind was just."

"I'm going to eat your tongue first," Cirisonna growled. She leapt forward, down from the elevated throne, upon the shield of the would-be king. Its silver burned in her chest, her lungs, and her knees gave out.

He swung the ax at the wolf, but Cirisonna swatted the blade away.

She snapped her jaws at his face, and he bashed the shield up under her chin. She yelped like a pained puppy and broke away from their entanglement.

The two of them circled around the room. Stepping carefully over some discarded body part or weapon. Neither willing to break eye contact.

"After I kill you," the prince threatened. "I'm going to burn every village in the valley until there is nothing left of your filth in all the world."

Cirisonna howled, attacked.

The prince lifted his shield to deflect the snarling, snapping jaws coming for his throat. And aimed to feed her the end of his ax instead. The weapon's blade missed Cirisonna's mouth but caught her under the eye. A chunk of black fur fell away and a wet red filled in the spot left behind. He swung the sword again, and Cirisonna caught the blade in her enormous hand. Before she could gain any purchase, the shield also came forward and bashed Cirisonna's teeth.

Enraged, Cirisonna grabbed the prince's shield and yanked it free from his arm. It was too heavy in her grip and her arm screamed in protest. It flew from her hand and skirted across the floor, skipping over pools of blood like a river stone, and lodged into the rubble of the broken doorway.

The clock bell rang, commandeering Cirisonna's attention. She yelped when the prince pulled the ax down through her grasp, severing two of her fingers. He thrust the blade toward her heart. It bit into her flesh, tasted her blood, but did not make its mark. The clock played percussion to the prince's spirited attack. His sword swung, cutting the air, and slicing into skin.

Cirisonna stepped backward until a paw hit a stair. She braced herself upon it. At the strike of five, she sprung forward with all her might, plowing him down onto his back. They skipped across the floor, colliding in a lake of blood. Just as the clock struck six, a splash of gore painted the brawny prince with legacy's end.

Cirisonna's clawed-hand lifted above her head and, swifter than a blade, those claws tore into the prince's chest and wrapped around his heart. A final spray of blood spat from the prince's lips. His eyes went wide, taking in the sight of his heart torn from his chest.

The clock struck nine and Luscious the crow came squawking into the throne room. He circled around Cirisonna's shoulders, urging her toward the throne.

"Shit," she said, a growl on the edge of her voice. *The throne.* She had to be sitting on the throne at midnight to hold up her end of the dark fairy's bargain.

Ten. Eleven. Cirisonna took her place. Luscious perched on her shoulder and nuzzled the fur on her cheek.

The clock struck twelve, and the moonlight peered through the skylight at the top of the dome. Its blue beams shrouded Cirisonna and the throne. Her black fur transformed into a black-silk gown. Claws became hands. Her face returned to its familiar shape. Even Luscious had become himself again and scurried into Cirisonna's hand.

"Well done," whispered a nowhere voice. A black mist settled upon the stairs before the throne. Her face covered in a stag's skull mask, the dark fairy materialized in a low bow at Cirisonna's feet. She stood straight and commanded Cirisonna to do the same. "You kneel to no man, Queen Cirisonna of the Black Wood. Protector of the forest. Victor of the Endless War."

The fairy raised her hands over their heads and,

clutched between them, appeared a bronze thorned crown. She lowered it upon Cirisonna's head. And once it settled, an invasive chill vined down Cirisonna's neck, into her shoulders, and across her chest.

The fairy's voice was in Cirisonna's head again. "Declare."

"I am the wolf, guardian of fear. And it is I, as Queen, who reigns dominion here."

The fairy bowed her head, and Cirisonna sat back upon the throne.

"So long as you protect the forest, the forest shall, too, protect you," said the fairy.

Cirisonna bowed her head. Luscious crawled to the armrest at Cirisonna's side and sat upright, beaming with pride. "And Luscious shall be my eyes in the sky, through the dark. And my ears, near the ground, through the day."

She pet his head and, at his signal, looked up. Peering through the window above her, a clear-sky sunrise began a new day.

Acknowledgments

Special thanks to donors who helped make this publication possible:

-Mazie -Kat -Natasha -Kota -Eve -Mike -Dennis -Bryce -Jae -Molly -Stephen -Richie -Shawn -Abby -Susan -Jennifer -Stefanie -John B.

Thank you to our friends at Inked in Gray Pub
inkedingray.com

And to our dear friend and author Stefanie Contreras
latinageekgirl.com

About the Authors

Some wonder what it's like in author Alexis L. Carroll's head after reading one of her stories. Imagine, if you can, a party where Trent Reznor, David Bowie, and Guillermo del Toro are the hosts while Alexis sits awkwardly in the corner jotting everything down. When not writing, she can be found in the salon creating colorful hair and swoopy fringe. Outside of multitasking careers, Alexis loves to explore new places and eat tasty food in the state of Oregon, where she lives with her mate, two doppelgangers, piranhas and hellhounds.

Join Alexis and her adventures @alexisxstetic

Amanda doubles her millennial angst by not only being a writer but also a visual artist; a painter in particular. She spends most of her time in existential conversation with her cats and watering her plants. Born and raised in Oregon, Amanda denies being a hipster but the blue hair and doc martins would argue otherwise. She collects swords and pens, and watches Lord of the Rings far more often than a normal well-adjusted person ought to.

Follow the journey across social media @BatwoMANDA

CONTENT WARNINGS

- Animal Attack: The Untamed Daughter, They'll Make Monsters of Us All, Greed
- Assault: The Untamed Daughter (implied)
- Blood / Descriptive gore: all stories
- Body Horror: The Untamed Daughter, The Girl Who Wasn't Fear, They'll Make Monsters of Us All
- Bullying: The Dealings of Thorns and Crows
- Cursing / Foul Language: all stories
- Death Ideation: The Untamed Daughter
- Decapitation: In The Trees
- Drugging: The Untamed Daughter, Greed
- Kidnapping: The Untamed Daughter, In the Trees
- Menstrual Blood: The Girl Who Wasn't Fear
- Murder: all stories
- Racism: Greed (hinted at)
- Religious Zealotry: The Girl Who Wasn't Fear
- War Images: They'll Make Monsters of Us All